To Overcome Betrayal

Sarah Lamb

ISBN: Paperback 978-1-960418-23-4
ISBN: Large Print 978-1-960418-24-1

Contents

May you always find the place you belong.

Chapter 1

1879, Spring Falls, Kansas

Evie Brown rubbed her clammy hands down the sides of her dress and hoped no one noticed. To say she was nervous was an understatement. The sitting room she had been invited into was larger than any she'd ever seen before. A vast stone fireplace, set but not lit, was in the middle of the room against a long wall.

The walls themselves were a warm-colored wood, and paintings—a mix of landscapes and still life—hung on them. Her eyes landed on one of the town, and she admired its likeness. The artist had captured the area beautifully. Tall amber grasses with small blue and purple flowers dotted in between, and in the distance, rolling hills. It was so realistic, Evie felt as though she could step inside it.

The entire room was designed with comfort in mind. Several plush chairs and a sofa were scattered about, along with round tables, a desk and straight-back chair, and lamps that rested throughout the room. Evie had never seen so many in her life. In the evenings, instead of being clustered around one or two small sources of light, the room could be fully illuminated if the owner wanted. Instead of eyes straining to make out words on a book's page or the eye on a needle, they'd be effortless in their evening's endeavors.

How pleasant it would be to spend time in a room such as this! Tall shelves of books filled a portion of the back room, and Evie wished she were closer to see what titles were upon them.

Footsteps sounded, drawing closer, and Evie took a deep breath, then another. She hoped she didn't look too nervous. She wouldn't want her interview to go poorly. Getting this job was crucial. There was no other choice, and no other jobs in town. She simply had to have this one. No matter she was terrified—both of the labor the job would demand and also the man she'd be working for. Her uncle depended on her, and she was going to do all she could to be sure she helped him.

"You are here for the interview?" a woman asked briskly.

Evie spun quickly. "Yes, ma'am. I am."

"Why don't you sit?" The woman motioned to one of the chairs.

Once Evie had, marveling at the soft cushion beneath her, the woman, somewhere in perhaps her fifties, with hair silvering at her temples and a serious expression on her face, gave her a long look. She must have liked what she saw, and nodded before speaking. "I'm Mrs. Staunton, the housekeeper."

"Evelyn Brown. But please call me Evie," she added quickly.

"You live in the boarding house, don't you, Miss Brown?" Mrs. Staunton asked.

"Yes, ma'am."

"And you are seeking employment here."

It wasn't a question, it was a fact. And the truth was, if there was any other option, Evie wouldn't be here. Not at Mr. Radcliffe's house. She'd heard things about the man, though she'd never seen him.

A girl who'd worked in his kitchen once whispered about how he was cruel. Always demanding perfection. Another boarder had talked about how he didn't care for anything but making money. The boarding house owner, Mrs. Wimple, had told them to stop gossiping, but then she'd added that Mr. Radcliffe was so wealthy, it was to be expected that he was those things and more.

Their words hadn't exactly made Evie feel any better about her prospects of asking for and getting the job, but with nothing else there in Cottonwood Falls, she'd either have to get this job or move to Spring Falls and search there, if she was to help her uncle.

"The job includes a room," Mrs. Staunton said. "All three meals, of course. Your duties would be that of a housemaid."

"What...what might those be?" Evie asked. She'd never done anything other than work in a shop, and hoped she'd be able to do all that was required of her.

"You'd be in charge of whatever tasks we have at the time on top of daily chores, such as dusting, sweeping, refreshing linens. Those sorts of things."

Mrs. Staunton folded her hands in front of her as she observed her, and Evie nodded. That didn't sound too bad.

"At times, you might be asked to help in the kitchen, but not often. You'd set the tables, perhaps bring dishes in. Run an errand. We have a cook and her helper. It's not too often your assistance will be needed, but it might happen. The laundry also gets sent out to a woman in the town. She comes once a week to pick it up. Seeing that it's all ready for her would be one of your tasks. She washes and folds it all. You'll simply put it away once it arrives." Mrs. Staunton paused. "I understand you have never done this kind of work before?"

"No, ma'am. Not outside of our house, anyway," Evie said. Then, she hurriedly added, "But I learn quickly and I work hard."

Mrs. Staunton nodded. "I'd expect nothing less," she said. "Mr. Radcliffe also depends on that. He seeks only to keep those in his employ who do a satisfactory job. There are times that he entertains others here for the weekend when he is doing business. The house must run well at all times."

"Yes, ma'am," Evie said. She wasn't sure how else to answer. Mrs. Staunton was giving her a considering look. Finally, she stood. Evie quickly did the same.

"Follow me, and I will give you a tour of the house," Mrs. Staunton said.

She walked out of the room without seeing if Evie was following. They went into the hallway, and Mrs. Staunton pointed out the various rooms. Evie was sure her eyes were as large as saucers. It seemed unimaginable to her that one man—and of course his staff—lived in such a large home.

The kitchen was enormous, as was the pantry. On the first floor, there was also a laundry room, the sitting room, a library, a private study which Mrs. Staunton said no one was allowed in but Mr. Radcliffe, Mrs. Staunton's small study, various closets where supplies were kept, and a large dining room.

Upstairs were six bedrooms and more closets with storage. The housekeeper paused before a door. "Mr. Radcliffe, of course, sleeps here on this floor, and this is his room. It's the largest. The other men sleep in the bunkhouse. There are currently eighteen ranch hands here, and they have their own cook. There are more hands in total, but several are out buying new cattle and horses."

"My goodness," Evie whispered. "I knew this place was large, but not that large."

"That's why it's on the outskirts of town," Mrs. Staunton said. "The other bedrooms on this floor are for guests who might visit."

She led Evie up another flight of stairs. There, she motioned to eight rooms and storage closets, smaller than those below. "These are for the female staff," Mrs. Staunton said, then pointed to the first door. "My room is here. Of course, I am only in it at night. If I'm not visible downstairs, I'm likely in my study doing the housekeeping records."

She pushed open the door next to hers. "This would be your room, should you accept the job."

A single bed, small chest, a chair and side table, square mirror the size of her hand, and some pegs along the wall were the entirety of the contents. "There's bedding in the closet," Mrs. Staunton said, pointing down the hall.

"It's more than satisfactory," Evie said as she walked into the room. It was true. Though a servant's room, it was larger than the one at her boarding house, and had a lovely view of the outdoor vegetable garden.

"Then you will take the position?" Mrs. Staunton asked.

Evie nodded. "I'd be grateful for it," she answered. And it was true. Her uncle's latest letter felt heavy through the pocket of her dress, and his desperate plea for help burned in her mind.

She would do all she could to save him from his dire state. There was no one else who could.

Chapter 2

"I'm so glad we could have dinner together," Ruth said as she gazed adoringly at Andrew across the small table.

The hotel's restaurant was the finest dining that Cottonwood Falls had to offer, and it wasn't too bad. No, it wasn't as fancy as other places he'd been, but it would do. Especially tonight. He was tired and longed to be in his study with a book and something warm to drink, relaxing.

Instead, politely, Andrew said, "I'm glad I got back in time."

"How did your business deal go?" Ruth asked.

"Like all the others." Andrew shrugged. "Closed it."

He wasn't wanting to brag, but it was true. He had both an eye and the aptitude for business. As such, he was one of the wealthiest people for miles around. Quite possibly one of the wealthiest in the entire state. He worked hard, though. Hard work was what it took in order to build up anything from scratch, and he had been building for years.

Ruth cleared her throat, and Andrew glanced at her. "My apologies," he said.

"Woolgathering?" she asked.

"No, just a little tired," he answered.

She fluttered her eyelashes coyly. "That's all right. I understand. Tell me about your day. What's made you so exhausted? Something on your mind? Or...someone?"

The candles flickered on the table, and before he could say anything, their meal arrived. Roast beef, mashed potatoes, string beans, and rolls. Andrew tucked into his dinner.

Ruth sighed and dragged her fork through the potatoes. When he didn't say anything, she sighed louder. Then cleared her throat.

"What's the matter?" he asked finally.

"I'm just tired," she said. "Tired of eating here. This is the nicest place in town, but it's getting dull eating the same meals each week. I'm also tired of this little town. I long to travel," she told him. "To see the world."

Something tightened inside of him. Comments like that always led to one place. At least, they had with all of the other women he'd known.

"Is that so? I enjoy staying home," he answered mildly. "My ranch keeps me busy, so I enjoy the rare quiet evening at home. Even better when it's not filled with paperwork."

"Oh, pish," Ruth answered, tossing her hair. "You have enough money to pay people to do all that for you. You could go traveling around. See the world. Buy more businesses."

"And hire people to run them for me, so I make more money and get even richer?" he asked dryly.

"Yes," she said, a bright smile on her face. "Isn't that what rich men do?"

"None of the ones I know," Andrew answered, buttering a roll. "They work hard. Out here in the West, we aren't like the fancy folks back East. We make our living by the sweat of our brow. Be it settling the land, raising it up, or creating jobs for others, we work hard. We don't have the luxuries that many back East have, nor the leisure time."

"That could change," Ruth said, "if you wanted it to. I think you just like being out here with all this dust and those cows and horses of yours."

She wrinkled her nose and waved her hand. "I mean, look at you! You are a wealthy man, and you dress like a ranch hand. Even tonight, though I see you at least tried to dress better, your clothes are older. Worn." Ruth picked up her fork and asked, "Don't you like me? Don't you want to see me happy?"

He stilled, the bite of mashed potatoes halfway to his lips. Slowly, he lowered his fork. "What a sudden question. One that feels a little too serious, considering we've only known each other a few weeks. Is this about how I dress or something else?"

Her pout, one he recognized by his vast experience with women as fictitious, pulled prettily on her mouth. "What's a few weeks or a few months when you know you've found the one you want to spend the rest of your life with?" she nearly purred. "When you know, you know."

Andrew released his sigh internally. He'd known the moment they met, him nearly knocking her down outside the general store, that the woman was trouble. But when he'd asked how he could make it up to her, and she'd asked him to take her to dinner, he'd obliged. And now wholeheartedly regretted it.

He didn't care one bit that her father owned the hotel, and that made her fairly well off. Perhaps that's why she'd suggested hiring people to run his businesses. That's what her father did. He'd only seen the man once. Did he ever get his hands dirty? It didn't matter. He wasn't interested in her. At all. But, in case he was wrong, that she wasn't just after him for what he had, he decided to ask and find out for himself.

Finishing his forkful, he cut a bite of beef and asked, "What is it about me that makes you know?"

Her giggle was loud. It grated on him, striking a certain tone that screeched in his ear, and Andrew knew he wouldn't be able to abide hearing it often.

"Why, the fact you are the most handsome man in town, and the richest. I'm the most beautiful woman in town, and also well off. Together, we make a fine couple, don't you think?" Ruth asked.

"I...don't, actually," Andrew answered her.

The shocked look on her face would have been gratifying for him, had it not been followed by a flash of anger. "Is that so?" she asked coldly.

"I don't plan to settle down with anyone," Andrew said calmly. "And this isn't the start of a relationship. I knocked you over, you said dinner would be an acceptable apology, and here we are. We've been enjoying each other's company as friends passing the time. Nothing more has been on my mind."

"Well! I never!" Ruth gasped. She sat up so suddenly that others in the dining room stared over at them when her chair nearly tipped backward.

"You're as horrible as everyone says," she sniffed, raising her chin.

"I am," he agreed. "Demanding, exacting—"

"Horrible!" she finished.

Andrew just shook his head. "You don't even know me," he said quietly. "Nor do you want to. You only like what you see, what you think I have. What I can give you."

Ruth's lip quivered. "You'll be sorry one day that you turned me down," she said, "when you're all alone, and I'm happy and married."

"I'm sure I will," he agreed, and took another bite. The potatoes weren't bad. More salt was needed, but there was a shaker. He could handle that himself.

When he looked up again, Ruth was gone. Though he should have felt relief, all Andrew felt as he paid for their meal, went to the livery for his horse, and rode home was weariness.

Though tonight's meal had happened at a much more rapid pace than usual, the outcome had been the same. Women only wanted him for his money. It wasn't that he was stingy. Far from it. Both anonymously and with his name attached, he'd given much to many causes. But for some reason, the fact that he was unmarried and wealthy was a combination that many women refused to accept. He was tired of them throwing themselves at him.

Almost as if they were passing him from one to another to see who could win his affection, it had gotten to the point that the women of the town didn't even pretend to be interested in him as an individual. After only a time or two of meeting each other, they'd all ask for something. Gifts, fancy meals, a ring on their finger.

"I've got her, Mr. Radcliffe," Joe, his stablemaster, said as he rode up.

"Thank you," Andrew answered.

"Long day?" Joe asked.

"Incredibly," Andrew replied. "It's good to be here at last." He clapped Joe on the shoulder and headed along the gravel path to the sanctuary of his home.

He strode toward the house and entered through the kitchen. Cook looked up from the dish she was washing when she saw him.

"Hungry?" she asked, moving to wipe her sudsy hands on her apron.

"Had dinner, but thank you," he answered, continuing through toward his study without slowing.

Mrs. Staunton was in the hallway, a stack of blankets on her arm. "Mr. Radcliffe," she said. She looked at him expectantly.

"Good evening," he told her as he paused. "Did you need me?"

"I simply wanted to let you know I've hired a new housemaid," Mrs. Staunton told him. "Expect to see a new face. Her name is Evelyn, but she prefers to be called Evie. She seems well mannered, and I hope she will be an asset to the household."

"Fine, fine. Whatever you think. I trust you unequivocally in these matters," he said.

"I appreciate your confidence. I think she'll do well," the housekeeper told him.

"Wonderful. Thank you." Andrew continued walking, then stopped. He could sense the housekeeper still staring at him. When he turned, there was a hesitation on her face that made him pause at his study door. "Is something wrong?" he asked. "Do you have doubts about her?"

"No, none about the girl," Mrs. Staunton answered quickly. "It's just you. I felt worried for a moment."

"About me?" Andrew asked.

"It didn't go well, did it?" she asked quietly.

Mrs. Staunton had been with him for nearly ten years. She was almost like a mother. It was impossible to hide anything from her.

"I never should have agreed to such a silly thing," he told her, shaking his head. He didn't mind admitting it.

"Why did you?" she asked, curious.

He sighed and shrugged. "I suppose... to prove to her, and myself, that she's not the one for me. Honestly, I'm not sure there is a woman out there for me, but every single one in Cottonwood Falls seems determined to throw themselves at me."

"There's one for you," Mrs. Staunton said firmly. "She might not be there in town, but there is one."

"Someone for everyone, eh? That's what they say?" Andrew grinned, but was sure it looked more like a grimace.

"That's right," she answered stoically.

He forced a smile. "Good night, Mrs. Staunton," he said, and went into his study, closing the door quietly behind him. Really, he didn't mind if he didn't find that someone. He was used to being lonely. It didn't mean he liked it, but he was used to it. And if you were used to something, it was easier to bear it.

Chapter 3

Evie let out a mumble of frustration as she stretched on the tips of her toes to reach the built-in shelves behind a small door above the doorway. No matter she had a low stool to stand upon, she still couldn't quite reach. Just another inch or two was all she needed.

Huffing in irritation, she glanced about for some way to reach the blanket she'd been asked to take to one of the bedrooms. Her gaze fell upon the duster she'd been carrying, and she grabbed it quickly, using the handle to pull a corner of the blanket closer. As it finally came within grasp of her fingertips, she lurched forward and grasped it. Triumph filled her.

"Evie," Mrs. Staunton said, and Evie nearly tumbled off the stool in surprise at her sudden appearance. "Have you forgotten you get the afternoon off?"

With a small gasp, Evie looked at her. "Oh! I had forgotten! Once I take the blanket where you asked, may I go?"

"Nonsense," Mrs. Staunton said. "You're such a hardworking girl." She shook her head, but her smile showed she wasn't upset. "I almost have to force you to take your breaks. I'll take it on my way."

"Thank you," Evie said. "If you are sure?" She then added softly, "I'm just grateful to be here, and don't wish to jeopardize my position."

"You are in no danger of doing so," Mrs. Staunton assured, and then left with the blanket, leaving Evie to shut the small door, replace the stool, and then nearly fly down the stairs and out into the sunshine.

Duties inside of the house usually kept Evie from enjoying the fresh air. While the house's windows were open, it wasn't the same thing as being outdoors, under the warm sun, blue sky, and small wisps of clouds. It was a beautiful day, and more than once, she'd looked longingly through the window. But now that she was out here, she was unsure what to do, and where she was allowed to go.

It would be too far to walk to town and back before it was dark. She also wasn't sure that she could find her way easily without getting lost. Deciding to wander within sight of the house, and find a place to read her book in the sunshine, Evie walked down a small path that led toward the stable. Perhaps the horses were out and she'd be able to watch them as she read.

Just as she reached the stable, it started to sprinkle. "Of all the times," Evie groaned, and she dashed in, seeking shelter. A ranch hand was just leaving, and she asked, "Excuse me, sir?"

"Joe," the man answered. "How can I help you?"

"It's my half afternoon off," Evie explained. "I was going for a walk when it started to rain. May I stay here until it stops?"

He nodded. "You can. You'll see a few of the horses in their stalls. Don't touch them. They aren't familiar with you, and I wouldn't want you to get hurt. I'll introduce you to them another time if you'd like, but just now I've got to get this saddle to someone to mend."

"I understand," Evie agreed. "Thank you."

Joe nodded and then walked out, the heavy looking saddle on his shoulder. Evie strolled around the barn, sniffing deeply. There was a distinct hay and horse smell. It wasn't unpleasant, though. The barn was quite clean for an outdoor building that housed animals. She took a moment to admire each of the horses as she walked past. They were stunning. Though she didn't know a great deal about horses, she knew that these must be some of the best around. Mr. Radcliffe depended on them to be.

Mrs. Staunton had told her part of his wealth was from cattle, the other from breeding horses. She wondered what the man was like. Though she'd been there nearly two weeks, she'd yet to meet him, but he seemed to be a successful rancher, and treated the people who worked for him fairly. That was reassuring, seeing as the others at the boarding house had her quite worried he'd be terrible. As she hadn't met him yet, she would reserve judgment, but the house seemed to run well, and there was no discontent inside.

Evie was grateful for that. She'd been concerned at first that she wouldn't be accepted by the other staff. So far, that hadn't been the case. Everyone had been polite, kind even.

Her circuit around the barn complete, Evie peered out the large open doors. It was still raining. Though it had turned into a gentle rain, it was still far too heavy for her to wander about or even dash to the house without getting soaked. She couldn't help but feel disappointed. It had been so beautiful out, without a cloud in the sky. It seemed quite unfair that it was sunny and raining.

She glanced about and found a low stool, then pulled it over near a window. She'd just sit and read until the weather cleared. Perhaps then she'd have time for a small walk and to see more of Mr. Radcliffe's property, so if Mrs. Staunton asked her to deliver a message to someone like she had yesterday, she'd better know where to go.

Her head low over the book, Evie tried to lose herself in the pages. Try though she might, worries crept in. They had a way of doing that when she wasn't working herself to near exhaustion. The book was soon forgotten. How was her uncle? Was he doing well? She'd be paid soon, and would send him all of it. Would that be enough until her next pay to see him through?

Her uncle was all she had. She simply had to help him. Evie stared out at the large house in the distance wistfully. If only she had all the money in the world, like Mr. Radcliffe seemed to. Surely, she'd not worry about a thing if that were the case. While she supposed rich people must have some problems, they wouldn't have the same ones that she did—making sure she had enough to support herself and her family.

As she let her eyes roam once more over the large house and then the stable, Evie shook her head. It was obvious Mr. Radcliffe had no problems at all. He was doing very well for himself.

Footsteps sounded, crunching along the stone pathway, and Evie glanced up, expecting Joe. However, it wasn't him. She'd never seen this ranch hand before. He was tall with dark hair, a lock of it falling into his dark eyes. Her heart started to thud. Who was he?

His eyes landed on her just then, and Evie nearly melted. She'd never had such a reaction before, but she'd also never stared into such warm eyes. Surely, she could be excused for her reaction this once.

The man paused just inside of the stable and brushed off some of the raindrops that clung to his arms. He frowned then, and her heart sank. Was she in trouble? Joe had said she could be there, but...

Nerves fueled her. Evie scrambled to her feet. "Hello," she managed to blurt. Before she could stop herself, she'd walked over to him and thrust out her hand. As he stared down at it, she continued, "Evie Brown."

Chapter 4

Andrew was deep in thought as he strode to the barn. It had been a long week. Ruth had sent two messages, both apologizing and asking him to meet her. He'd ignored the first one, then sent a note with the second, telling her that nothing he had said had changed, and he wished her good luck and the chance to travel. He had the feeling if he didn't send some sort of a reply, she'd simply send another note. Or show up in person. Thankfully, there had not been a third message.

As he glanced down at his worn shirt, the pants forming a hole near the knee and boots caked in muck, he nearly laughed. If she hadn't cared for him cleaned up at dinner, what would she think about him now?

He'd given up on the idea of a wife one day, and decided that he'd simply settle for companionship. That was all he needed. It wouldn't be with Ruth, though. He needed someone who wouldn't ask for everything under the sun. Someone who would help him not feel so lonely.

Though a soft rain was falling, he knew it wouldn't last long and planned to saddle his favorite horse and go for a ride to check on the fences being built in the north pasture. They were due to be finished within a week for a new herd of cattle, and he needed to make sure everything was on schedule.

Andrew stopped when he saw a flicker of movement he wasn't expecting inside the barn. There was a woman sitting and reading. He didn't recognize her, but judging by the dress she was wearing and the low bun she had on her head, she was a housemaid. Perhaps even the new one. Evelyn, was it?

He frowned as he stepped forward, ready to ask her if she was shirking her duties, when she saw him, quickly stood, and offered her hand. He was so surprised, he reached for it without even realizing, until his larger hand closed around her soft one.

"Hello. Evie Brown," she told him. "I'm new here, and it's my half afternoon off. I asked the man here earlier, Joe, if I could wait out the rain in the barn."

Andrew studied her. She had long, light brown hair, a spray of freckles across the bridge of her nose, and a friendly expression on her face. She also seemed a little nervous, as if she were worried he'd be upset she was there.

He quickly erased his frown. That likely wasn't helping the situation.

"Hello," he replied as he let go of her hand. "Nice to meet you."

She smiled at him, then asked, "Have you worked here long? I'm still learning everyone and everything."

He startled at the question. Work here? Didn't she know who he was? His mouth opened to correct her, when something made him close it again. Of course. They'd not met until now. Mrs. Staunton had been the one to hire her. He started to answer her, but when the reply came, it wasn't what he'd expected himself to say.

"I've been here a while."

"How do you like it?" she asked, with an open curiosity that surprised him. He wasn't used to such pointed questions, especially when they were directed at him. Most women hinted around at what they wanted to ask. But she didn't realize he was her employer. Andrew was sure that if she had known, her tone and questions and mannerisms would have been very different.

"Ah, I like it," he answered. "What about you?"

"It is better than I expected," she told him. "I was quite nervous starting here. Well, honestly, I still am. However, that fades a little each day that passes."

"Understandable," Andrew said. He peered outside. The rain was lessening. Good. He wanted to leave before he said something to give himself away. Dishonesty could lead to problems later. He'd already said something he might regret. He had to make sure not to run into this maid again.

"What's your name?" Evie asked. She came closer to him. "Aren't these horses magnificent? Mr. Radcliffe is so fortunate to have them!"

"Andrew," he answered. "And I agree. Each of these horses is incredibly special." He reached over and rubbed the forehead and nose of Ginger, a mare who had as spicy of an attitude as her name might suggest.

He could feel Evie watching him, but when he glanced over, the longing in her eyes was directed to the horse.

"Is she as silky as she looks?" Evie asked.

"Here," Andrew said, stepping to the side slightly. "Feel for yourself. "

"Oh, no. I can't," she said, much to his surprise. She squeezed her hands into fists and held them rigidly at her sides. Her eyes never left Ginger. "I want to. Just Joe told me not to."

He felt an appreciation at her words. The horses were a temptation for most anyone, so the fact that she'd obeyed spoke volumes about her character.

"That's because we have a few here who are aggressive," he told her. "But I'm with you. I'll let Joe know, if he says anything, that I allowed you."

She hesitated, but then nodded. Almost shyly, she stepped closer. Andrew caught the faintest of whiffs of orange coming from her. It was so unexpected, so delightfully fresh, he caught himself as he leaned in closer to sniff again, and moved back. Luckily, patting Ginger provided the perfect excuse.

"This is Ginger," Andrew said. "Let her smell your hand."

Evie did as he told, and once the mare had gotten her scent, gently rubbed the mare's nose, and let her hand glide down her long neck. "Such a beauty," she said.

Without meaning to, Andrew found himself observing her as she admired Ginger. Evie seemed so happy and relaxed. She was such a contrast from just about—no, from every—woman he'd ever known. She wasn't trying to impress him or acting like a damsel in distress. She was just herself. It was refreshing.

Evie withdrew her hand and asked, "Are you sure I won't get in trouble? Maybe I shouldn't have done that." She bit her lip in worry, and her brow furrowed as she glanced at him.

"It's fine," Andrew assured her. "I promise."

She released a breath. "Good. I'm a little nervous still, being new, and hope I won't make mistakes. I need this job and don't want to risk it." She looked fondly at Ginger. "Even for one as stunning as you are."

"What makes you need it?" Andrew asked. "If I'm not prying, that is."

"Oh, you aren't," Evie told him in that frank way she had of speaking. "I send my pay—well, I will once I get it—to my uncle who raised me. He's going to lose his house and business if I don't."

"Is that so? What kind of business does he have?" Andrew asked.

"He repairs things," Evie said. "A handyman. Truthfully, I don't know how he's managed until now, but I have to help him. He's the only family I have and depends on me."

"That's very noble of you," Andrew said. "You have a kind heart."

"He had the same when he took me in," Evie said. "I'd be an orphan without him." She paused, and worried her bottom lip between her teeth again. "I guess I am anyway, but I felt less lonely growing up with him nearby."

Evie shrugged then and said, "I don't want to sound like I'm complaining. I don't mean to, in any case. But you see now why I don't want to make any mistakes here. This job isn't just for my sake, but also that of my uncle. I don't want to disappoint him by only thinking about myself in the moment."

Andrew nodded, but before he could say anything, Evie glanced through the barn door. "Goodness. I think it's getting late. I'd best go back to the house and see what help is needed for dinner. It was good to meet you," she said, pushing a strand of her hair behind an ear. "I hope that I'll get to see you again sometime."

She started to the door, and Andrew said, "I hope that as well."

It was true, he realized as he watched her scurry down the path in the direction of the house. For some reason, he liked her.

Was it the way she spoke as though they were equals? That she hadn't recognized him? Maybe it was just that he sensed she had a good heart. Andrew wasn't sure. But he couldn't help but wonder when their paths would cross again.

Ginger snorted and shook her head. Andrew laughed. "I agree, girl. What have I gotten myself into? But..." He let his eyes linger outside where Evie had been just a moment before. "But I find myself unexpectedly liking her and wanting to see her again. I'm not sure the last time I felt such a combination in someone. Especially a woman."

He set to work saddling Ginger and then led her outside. As they rode to the north pasture, he found that his thoughts kept wandering to the girl who smelled of oranges. Each time, he pushed them away, even though he knew they'd come back just a moment later. It wasn't unpleasant.

Chapter 5

"Put two rolls and some butter on that plate," Cook said to Evie. She nodded with her head, her hands full—a plate in one and a thick slice of meatloaf on a serving spoon in the other.

"Anything else?" Evie asked, eyeing the tray.

Cook set the plate down and shook her head. "It's all there. Wait. Add one more napkin. Just in case."

Evie got one, folded it neatly, set it on the tray, and then hefted it into her hands. She'd been asked to take Mr. Radcliffe his dinner. He was eating in his study, as he often did.

"Just set it out on the small table outside of the study, knock, and then leave it there," Mrs. Staunton said. "He'll get it when he has a moment."

"Yes, ma'am," Evie said, and walked through the kitchen door, down a hallway, through the foyer, and to the hallway that would lead to Mr. Radcliffe's study. She wondered if she'd see him today. Not once had she spotted him, and her imagination was starting to run wild.

Was he as old as her uncle? Perhaps a little younger? A gruff man with a large mustache? For a man who seemed demanding—at least according to those in the boarding house—he didn't seem to have an ego, for there were no portraits of him hanging in the large home.

Evie slid the tray onto the table, knocked at the study door, and called, "Your dinner is here, sir."

Though she wanted to stay to see if he'd peek out, she knew that wouldn't be appropriate of her. It also might risk her job, so she left, scurrying back the way she'd come.

Next time I see Andrew, I'll ask him about Mr. Radcliffe, she decided. *After all, he's been here a great deal longer than me. Perhaps the men see him more often, since they work outdoors and that's his business.*

Evie wondered when she might see him again. Hopefully, it wouldn't be too long before she did. Though their interaction had been short, she sensed he was a kind person. He'd likely not mind her questions.

She was so curious about Mr. Radcliffe, but Mrs. Staunton had made it clear that she didn't abide gossip in the house. It was a good rule, in truth. Idle tongues often led to idle hands, as well as tension and discontentment within a household. But she couldn't help but wonder. The longer she went without seeing him, the more she couldn't help but imagine.

Was Mr. Radcliffe hunched over? Did he walk with a cane? Perhaps...perhaps Mr. Radcliffe wasn't a man at all. Might he be a woman, who did business under a male's name, as that was the only way that she could? The idea was exciting, but Evie had the feeling, as soon as she thought it, that it wasn't true.

No, Mr. Radcliffe was obviously a man. Whenever she drew near the study, there was a distinct scent of leather and hay and horse. It wasn't bad, though. Such a smell spoke of his hard work, and that had to make him a good man, surely. It seemed he joined his men in the labor, instead of directing it all from behind a desk. That was a good trait in a person, and one she could admire.

A few hours later, Evie was all yawns when she finally got to retire to her room. She rubbed her eyes, took out a sheet of paper and a pencil, and sat down to write her uncle.

Dear Uncle,

I am enclosing my pay in hopes that it will both help and be of comfort to know that I am doing all that I can to assist you. I do not mind my job, though it is tiring. I help about the house, run small errands on the ranch when one of the ranch hands isn't nearby, and I also assist in the kitchen near mealtimes.

Though I've never met him, Mr. Radcliffe seems to be a fair employer, as my pay is reasonable, the housekeeper is kind to me, and I was given a room of my own, along with my meals. Every Sunday, I get the morning off, and I get a half afternoon every ten days. It seems to be a reasonable arrangement, and so far it is working out well.

Evie tapped the pencil to her lips. What more should she write? She knew she was not going to tell him about Andrew. That was her own cherished secret. Just remembering how close they'd stood in the barn, how kindly he'd spoken to her when she wanted to see Ginger, made her heart beat a little quicker with excitement.

Evie had stood near plenty of men. After all, she'd worked in a shop, lived in a boarding house, and had been to events where she'd chatted with men. But not a single one had ever made her feel nervous or fluttery or hopeful that she'd see him again soon. And that he'd liked her. She very much hoped she'd made a good impression upon Andrew.

Andrew had smelled much the same as when she'd walked past Mr. Radcliffe's study—leather, hay, and horses. But then, each of the men here must smell like that. Evie shook her head and smiled. She was being so silly. She was simply a maid. There was no future in the lofty hopes that went through her mind.

But...he was a ranch hand, wasn't he? Not much difference. They both worked. Besides, they could just be acquainted. What was wrong with that? She longed to have a friend, and perhaps one day a male friend who would be more. Would that be Andrew?

The moment she wondered, she frowned. "Of course not," she mumbled, and set herself overtop the letter again. "We hardly know each other. What a foolish thing for me to ponder on. I'm here to work and help my uncle. Not get mixed up in anything more than a friendship."

I am terribly tired, so will keep this letter short, she continued writing, *but please know that I love you, and as soon as I receive my next pay, I will post it the following day and do all that I can to help you. Do not lose hope, Uncle, for all will be well. I sense it.*

Your loving niece,

Evie

She folded the letter carefully, placed it into an envelope, and set it near her bedroom door. Tomorrow, she'd see if she could go to town to post it. If not, one of the ranch hands would likely be going. She'd give him the money for the postage.

Evie brushed out her long hair, put on her nightgown, and crawled into bed. She was so tired, she felt sure she'd fall asleep the moment her head hit the pillow. However, that wasn't what happened. She fell asleep, but was restless, as one nightmare after another raced through her mind. First, her uncle was huddled outside of his shop, destitute and crying out for her as an evil-looking man nailed boards across his shop door.

Then, her uncle stood, angrily shouting at her. "You! You did this. It is you who has made me suffer. Why didn't you help me?"

Evie tried to tell him she had tried, wanted to speak and beg his forgiveness, explain that she was doing all she could, but the words wouldn't form. Black clouds billowed overhead, and the skies burst open, nearly drowning her. Evie feared she'd be washed away.

Part of her knew she was dreaming, and she tried to struggle awake, but was unable to, the nightmare too powerful. Just as she thought the tears streaking down her cheeks would never fade, a man on a horse raced in, swept her up, and carried her away.

Evie gasped, feeling the wind rushing, two strong arms around her, and smelling leather, hay, and horse. She turned, trying to see the face of the rider, and then she woke.

Sitting up, Evie pressed a hand to her heart, trying to slow the thumping. It had all felt so real. She closed her eyes and drew in a shuddering breath. Her poor uncle. She was doing all she could, and hoped he knew that. And Andrew...was he the man on the horse? She'd only just met him, so how was it she dreamed of him?

Though she'd not complain in the least if he were to one day confess his affection toward her, Evie reminded herself she'd be content simply to call him a friend. She shouldn't be fixated on someone she'd just met. No matter being around him had felt so comfortable.

She settled back against her pillow, thinking of their singular conversation and how much she'd enjoyed it. Before she knew it, the rooster was crowing, the sun was dawning, and it was time to get out of bed.

A flicker of movement caught her eye as she was pinning her hair back, and Evie glanced out the window. There, striding out of the house, was Andrew, purpose in his step. He must have been sent on an errand for Mr. Radcliffe. Evie couldn't stop the smile that came to her lips, nor the hope that she'd run into him again soon.

As much as she'd tried to pretend friendship would be enough, Evie couldn't help but wish for more one day.

Chapter 6

"This new group of cattle looks good, Boss," Joe said. He tucked his thumbs into his belt and added, "They sold you some fine specimens."

"Indeed." Andrew nodded. He let his gaze roam over the herd. It was good to see such quality stock filling the north pasture. Some of the finest cattle around, and now his to breed, sell, and profit from. He'd especially done well this last year, and some of the money was being used to build small houses on his land for a few of his men who wished to settle down and marry.

His men worked hard, and he wouldn't deny any of them a chance at happiness or a family, even if he knew he'd never have that. It was a good business practice too, he'd told himself to ease the pang of hurt over what he didn't have. Content workers made for ones who stay.

After a few instructions to Joe, Andrew set off toward the barn. He'd walked to the pasture instead of going on his usual ride. He'd spent so much time in the saddle the last week, walking was welcome. Still, he didn't want Ginger to think he was ignoring her, and decided to stop in at the barn on his way to his study.

There was a mountain of correspondence to go through, and he would, but a few moments of relaxation in his busy day was needed. It was something he'd had very little of as of late. Each morning, he left at dawn. The nights he made it home for dinner he was grateful.

The only good thing about being so tired was he didn't have to sulk about his own house, trying to avoid the new housemaid. He still didn't know what had possessed him not to admit to her who he was. At the time, he hadn't thought about the potential awkwardness of the situation.

Only that it was kind of nice being mistaken for a ranch hand. It let him relax. Be himself. Not have someone think that he could give them something or do something for them because of who he was. It was also nice not to have someone feel intimidated, as he felt Evie might have been.

He approached the barn and, to his surprise, saw her wandering his way, coming from another path. She caught sight of him and smiled, then waved. "Hello!"

Though she was the last person Andrew expected to see, her cheerful expression made him grin in return. "Hello," he answered. "What are you doing out here?"

"I was sent with a supply list to give to Mud," she answered, referring to the bunkhouse cook whose coffee was so thick, it had become his signature drink.

Andrew nodded. "Nice day," he offered, unsure what else he could say, and what he could do to get her to stay there for a few more moments with him.

"It is," she said, turning her face up toward the sky for a moment. "Makes me wish I had more outside chores."

"Still getting along well?" he asked.

She nodded. "I am. I enjoy the job, even if it's exhausting."

Exhausting. He'd have to ask Mrs. Staunton about that. Andrew's brows drew together. Did he expect too much from the household staff? Or did she? He knew the duties and workload of the ranch hands better than those of the women inside. That...might not be fair. Those women worked just as hard. In different ways, to be sure, but he needed to be certain they had enough hands for all the jobs around the ranch, both indoors and out.

"You look tired," Evie said softly as she stepped a little closer.

"I am," Andrew admitted. "I've had some long days. Dawn to midnight, a few nights."

"Mr. Radcliffe works you really hard," she said. He didn't miss the worried expression on her face. "I'm not sure if that's right."

"It's my own fault," he quickly assured her. "There are just some things I'd rather do on my own than ask someone else to do, if that makes sense."

She nodded slowly, but didn't look convinced. Andrew wasn't quite sure why, but he felt touched that she was concerned about him, and also worried that their boss—himself—was working him too hard. It was true, he expected a lot from himself. More than from others. But that's how he'd always been.

"I'm heading to the barn for a moment to see Ginger," he told her. "Want to join me?"

"Oh, I'd love to," she said, then gave a grimace toward the house. "But Mrs. Staunton expects me."

"You're a diligent worker," Andrew said. "I'm sure it's greatly appreciated."

"I hope so," she said with a sigh. "You never know, sometimes."

"I'm sure Mrs. Staunton sees just what you do," he assured her. "She is an astute woman. When is your next half day?"

"Tomorrow."

"Do you ride horses?" he asked. "That is, if you have no plans?"

Evie shook her head, and a long strand fell into her eyes. He almost reached forward to brush it out of her face, but quickly redirected his hand to his own hair.

"I've always wanted to," she told him. "Uncle didn't have one. We always walked if we needed to go somewhere, or borrowed a neighbor's wagon. And no, I've no plans at all."

"Meet me here tomorrow, then," Andrew told her. "I'll teach you how."

Evie's eyes widened. "Really? Oh, but surely that wouldn't be allowed. I mean...the horses here are all so valuable. I don't think Mr. Radcliffe would approve." She looked disappointed. "Thank you, though."

"Never mind about him," Andrew said, regretting he'd ever misled her. She was so concerned with acting appropriately, it made it difficult to do the things he was used to doing. "It'll be fine. I promise. I'll get permission."

"You will?" She looked doubtful.

"Yes. It's important you learn. What if there's an emergency and Mrs. Staunton needs you to go to town? It will take you too long to walk there."

Evie bit her lip, and he found his eyes drawn there. "I never thought of that," she admitted.

"Trust me. Meet you tomorrow?" he asked, pulling his eyes up to hers.

She nodded, and her face lit up. "Yes. But make sure you get permission. If it's a no, then I'm happy just to meet with you for a little, if you've nothing else to do."

"Wouldn't miss it for anything," Andrew said.

She started walking away, but turned back and grinned at him. He watched until she was out of sight, his weariness suddenly gone. He looked forward to tomorrow, looked forward to spending time with Evie.

He whistled and walked into the barn. Ginger was there and he spent a few moments with her. As he was getting ready to leave, Joe came in, holding a set of reins. Andrew hesitated, then he said, "Joe, there's a new housemaid."

"Met her," Joe said. "Seems a sweet girl."

"I'm...going to teach her to ride," Andrew admitted, feeling a little embarrassed at the admission. "There's nothing inappropriate going on. But..." He stopped. How was he going to say it? "She..." He stopped again. What was wrong with him?

But before he could spit out the words, Joe's jaw dropped. "She don't know who you are, does she?" he asked.

Andrew shook his head no.

"What'd you go and do that for?" Joe asked. He shook his head.

"It happened by accident," Andrew sighed. "And then things went too far. Can I count on you to keep my secret?"

Joe looked thoughtful. "For a time," he said. "But you'll need to tell her one day, and the longer you wait, the harder it's going to be for her and for you."

Andrew knew Joe was right. But he wasn't ready. Not yet. He was going to just have to hope that nothing happened to make her find out accidently. He wanted to spend time with her. Be Andrew, not Mr. Radcliffe, or Andrew Radcliffe, the wealthy rancher.

If the day ever did come, he just hoped she'd understand.

Chapter 7

Evie peered out her window at the full moon hanging in the sky. It lit up the entire ranch. She could see pastures, small buildings, and specks she knew to be animals. Shadows fell near the few trees, and she felt impatient. Sleep wouldn't come, no matter that she was tired. Excitement filled her as she eagerly waited for the afternoon ahead.

Riding! Andrew was going to teach her how to ride a horse! She wondered which of the magnificent animals she'd be allowed to try. Mrs. Staunton had told her that there were perhaps forty or fifty horses on the ranch, a number that astounded her, but made sense as each of his men likely had one, some were for breeding, and others were for sale.

Evie did hope that it would be a mild horse. Perhaps one very old and tame, not irritated with age. She hoped it wouldn't be too high up, and that Andrew would be right near her in case she were to fall.

A flutter went through her stomach, and then a warmth at the thought of him. It was so incredibly kind of him to teach her. She hoped that he was truthful, that he wouldn't get into trouble and neither would she. This job paid more than she was likely to get anywhere else. Especially if Mr. Radcliffe turned out to be unsatisfied by her and didn't give a reference or blackened her name.

She needed this job and couldn't afford to risk her uncle's livelihood or wellbeing, all because she was being selfish and doing something that she wanted to do.

Evie desperately hoped that scenario wouldn't ever be the case. She also hoped that she didn't make a fool of herself on the horse. How humiliating it would be if she were to fall!

Though she was sure she'd never be able to calm down and close her eyes, Evie was asleep just moments later. Thankfully, nightmare free. She'd never slept so poorly before, but it all manifested from the worries about her uncle, she was sure.

The next morning, Evie completed her tasks, and it was all she could do not to skip down to the stable, where she hoped Andrew would be. Sure enough, she found him and he grinned at her. "Hello!"

"Hello," she said, slightly out of breath from walking so quickly. "I'm so excited to be here!"

He laughed, then said, "We have a small problem, but only if you aren't okay with it."

She furrowed her brows. "What is the matter?"

"I couldn't find a sidesaddle," Andrew apologized. "By the time I realized, it was too late to go and borrow one from someone in town."

"Oh! Is that all?" Evie asked. She waved her hand dismissively, and lifted the hem of her skirt slightly. "I'm wearing thick stockings, so it shouldn't be too improper if I climb over."

"Then that's what we will do," Andrew agreed. "I promise not to stare."

She laughed as she noticed him quickly look away as his face reddened, and then watched eagerly as he picked up a pair of reins and headed toward a stall. "Who will I ride?"

"I thought I'd give you Starlight," Andrew said. He motioned to a black mare with an almost perfect star on her forehead.

"She's lovely," Evie said, hushed.

A lump of emotion came to her throat, and her eyes pricked with tears. This all suddenly felt too much. A riding lesson on a beautiful horse, the complete attention of a man she couldn't help but like, the perfect weather and...it felt almost too good to be true.

"You are sure we won't get into trouble?" Her voice wobbled, and she squeezed her hands together, slightly embarrassed, but concerned all the same.

Andrew reached over and rested one hand on top of hers. His eyes were warm and caring. "It's not a problem at all," he told her reassuringly. "Joe already knows."

The words made her feel better, and her shoulders relaxed. If Joe knew, then it must be acceptable. "Very well, then. What do I do?"

"I've already got Starlight saddled," Andrew told her as he finished putting the reins on the horse. "We'll start simple. You'll climb on, and I'll walk next to you." He pointed a short distance away. "There's a mounting block there."

Evie walked toward it and waited as Andrew approached with the horse. Nerves fluttered throughout her, making her hands feel tingly with worry. The moment to get on this enormous beast had arrived. No matter she was beautiful and Evie wanted to climb on her.

Please don't let me make a fool of myself.

"Step up, and put your foot into the stirrup," he instructed her. "Hold on to the saddle. Now, swing your other leg up and over while you pull yourself up."

Doing as he told her, Evie was rewarded by successfully mounting the horse. Once in the saddle, she froze. "It's...rather high up," she gulped.

"You'll get used to it very quickly," Andrew assured her. "I'm going to start walking now, okay? I'm holding her and won't let go. You'll be safe. She's old and prefers to walk."

Evie nodded. "Okay." She gripped the saddle horn and held herself stiffly.

"It's okay to relax," Andrew told her. "I won't let anything happen to you. I promise you."

He led them slowly down the path toward one of the pastures. After a few moments, Evie unclenched her fingers. When nothing bad happened, she relaxed a little further. Soon, she was quite enjoying the slight sway underneath herself, and the view from several feet higher.

"Doing okay?" Andrew asked.

"Yes. I am," Evie answered happily.

"Good. We'll stop up ahead, and I'll help you off, and you can lead her around."

True to his word, they stopped a few minutes later. Andrew led Starlight next to a fence. "Put your foot here," he told her, "and then just slowly let yourself down."

Once Evie was back on the grass, he offered her the reins. "We'll walk together," he told her. "But you lead her."

Feeling a little more confident now than she had earlier, Evie took the reins and set out. She was relieved when the horse walked behind her and didn't balk. Andrew fell into step next to her, and there was a comfortable silence.

"You're doing well," Andrew commented after a short time.

"Thank you, and thank you for this," Evie said, glancing back at the horse. "I'm having a wonderful time. I almost feel guilty about it."

"Then let's do it again soon," Andrew said. "You shouldn't feel the least bit guilty."

"I'd like that," she answered.

There was silence again for a little, then he asked, "So, tell me about your uncle. You must love him very much to be working as hard as you do."

"I do," Evie said. "He's the only parent I've ever known. Mine died when I was a baby. I was too small to remember them. Uncle took me in, and has fed, clothed, and provided for me since. So, helping him in his hour of need is the least I can do."

"He's a lucky man," Andrew said. "I don't know too many people who would help family like that."

Evie looked surprised. "I'm sorry for that," she said. "You must not know the right kind of people."

Andrew grew a thoughtful expression on his face. "I might not," he agreed. "There are too many people only out for themselves, and those seem to be a good number of people I know."

"It's human nature," Evie said slowly as she continued to lead Starlight. "At the same time, it's also a terrible way to be."

They were quiet for a few steps, then she asked, "Where do you work at on the ranch?"

"All over," Andrew said. "I'm not sure there's an area I don't know."

"It's a large place," Evie said. "I'm sure that your help is appreciated."

He was quiet again, seemingly reflecting on her words. "I hope so," he finally said. "There are many seasons in life where you work hard and it's not noticed or appreciated."

Evie understood. But she felt sad that he might be feeling that way. She stopped and faced him. "I am sure that is not the case for you."

Andrew smiled, though it was a little bitter. "Even if it is, that's how it goes at times," he said. "Now. How about I help you back on, and I lead you again?"

She nodded, and once she was on Starlight's back, Andrew led her along a trail that fed back to the barn. She was a little sad the afternoon ride was over, but the sun was starting to dip, and she'd be needed back at Mr. Radcliffe's house.

"Thank you," Evie said as she tried to climb down.

Two hands wrapped around her waist, helping to lower her gently. They didn't pull away. Their eyes met, and Evie struggled to breathe. Everything around them felt so far away, and she wondered, for the briefest of moments, if he might lean in to kiss her.

What would she do if he did? Would it overly complicate things? Risk her job? Evie had just about decided she didn't care. That for one more moment she'd let herself enjoy whatever happened without guilt, when the sound of someone whistling and the crunching of footsteps on the stone sounded, and Andrew stepped back.

Chapter 8

Andrew stopped in front of the large window and watched as Evie, oblivious to his observation, hurried somewhere on an errand.

"Mail for you, Mr. Radcliffe," Mrs. Staunton said, startling him as she approached. "I've put it on the desk in your study."

"Thank you," Andrew said as he nodded and continued down the hallway. Had she seen him watching Evie? He hoped not. His stomach chose that moment to growl, and he stopped and turned. "Can I trouble you for a tray? I'll eat in my study tonight."

"Yes, sir," she answered, and walked in the direction of the kitchen.

Andrew winced when he opened the door to his study and saw the pile of mail. It was just as large as he'd expected.

Hopefully, none of it was something that would take him away from the ranch. He was tired of traveling. He needed to attend to his business, and also looked forward to glimpses here and there of Evie.

Evie. Her name made him smile, and he remembered how very serious her expressions were as she was both riding and leading Starlight. He also remembered how close she was when he'd helped her down. She'd smelled as before, of sweet oranges, and he assumed it must be her soap. He would never tire of that sweet scent.

They'd both startled as someone had interrupted what had felt like an intense moment. It was likely good that person had, or he might have kissed her. He'd wanted to. Felt like he was about to. She hadn't stepped back or pulled away. Did that mean if he'd asked her for a kiss, she'd have said yes?

Andrew took a deep breath, picked up the pile of mail, and started sorting it. He couldn't let himself think such a thing. It wasn't proper. She was his employee, and she was focused on helping her uncle. Not on starting a relationship with anyone.

There was a knock on his door—Mrs. Staunton, no doubt. "Come in," he said.

The door opened just enough for her to walk inside. She set down the tray and asked, "Anything else?"

"No, that's all," he told her. "Thank you."

After she left, Andrew picked up another letter and froze. This name he recognized. It wasn't one he'd thought of for a long time. Rosalee. She was tall, dark-haired, and incredibly good looking. She also knew it. Daughter of a wealthy cattle baron, she entertained frequently. This was an invitation to a dinner party in three days.

I do hope you'll come, it read. *An idea has come to mind I wish to discuss with you.*

Andrew was curious. He didn't really want to attend the dinner, but he had the feeling if Rosalee had a question and he didn't go there, she'd come out here, and that was the last thing he wanted.

If he thought about it, he wasn't sure why that was. Was it that he didn't want Evie to see her? Didn't want word to get around that he had a woman stopping by? It wasn't that he disliked Rosalee. They were friends, nothing more. But...he just didn't want her here.

Though he hoped the hands around the place wouldn't talk, he was sure they would. The fact he'd never married, though he had many attractive women seek him out, raised more than a few eyebrows. If nothing else, Rosalee was a woman anyone would talk about if they saw her. Knowing her, she was likely trying to get him to agree to something he didn't want to do. That was her way.

He sighed, and leaned forward to drop his head into his hands, elbows planted firmly on the desk. Then, he straightened, looked at the note again, and stood.

* * *

Andrew glanced around as he rode up to Rosalee's house in his carriage. It had taken nearly two hours to ride there, and it appeared she had a good number of visitors.

Her family's house was twice the size of his. Her father was rarely home, so she and her mother took to entertaining to keep themselves busy. It was about all they did. They had a staff of a dozen for the house, and he wondered if Rosalee had ever done a single thing for herself. Years before, he'd asked her that, and she'd laughed so hard tears had sprung to her eyes. But she'd never answered.

As the carriage slowed, a man in a servant's outfit approached. "Park that for you? I'll see to your horse," he added.

"Thank you," Andrew said as he climbed down. He walked up the staircase leading to the house. Music played. He didn't know what it was, only that he heard some stringed instruments.

Originally from back East, Rosalee and her mother refused to completely settle in the West, and kept many of their fancy ways, refusing to embrace what Rosalee called the uncivilized ways of the area. She preferred classical music to that of what was common in the West—fiddles, harmonicas, and an upbeat sound that set toes tapping.

He entered, and a cloud of perfume made his eyes water. Two arms wrapped tightly around his neck before they pulled away. "Andrew! Darling! It's been too long. A year, at least," Rosalee said.

"About that," Andrew agreed. He smiled at her. "You look much the same. Still lovely as ever."

It was true, so there was no reason not to say it. After he and Rosalee had decided they were not well suited for each other, they'd stayed friends. It had been perhaps four years now.

"What was it you wanted to talk to me about?" he asked.

"You've only just gotten here." Rosalee pouted as she took his arm. "Business already?"

"Is it business?" Andrew asked, curious. "With your father?"

She shrugged. "In a way. Walk with me, darling."

Rosalee looped her arm through his and led him toward the edge of the room, then through two doors that opened to a porch. Fresh air filled his nostrils and helped clear the perfume from all of the women inside.

"Much better," she said with a sigh once they were out of the noisy room. "I can hear you properly. So, tell me, how are you? You look good. Is that a new shirt?"

"Doing well," Andrew answered as he took in the potted flowers and extra chairs that had been set out on the porch. "Still busy. Working hard. And yes, since this sounded like something important, I tried to dress up a little more."

She laughed. "Same old Andrew. More comfortable in your work clothes. I'm glad you are doing well. But you've not settled," she said, quick to the point.

"Nor have you," he pointed out.

She laughed and tossed her head back. "You know why. There's no one I want. No one who can give me what I want."

He did. Though unmarried women had more societal and legal powers here in the West, it didn't mean that an unmarried woman could have all she wanted.

Rosalee faced him, and he saw it. The sharp, businesslike gaze of a predator. She'd always been that way. Sweet, shy, and flirtatious, but at the drop of a hat, cool, conniving, and determined to get what she wanted.

"What is it you want?" Andrew asked warily. There was a slight regret running through him that he'd come, but his curiosity outweighed that.

"I have a proposition for you," she said.

"I'm listening. Doesn't mean I'll say yes, but I'm listening."

She nodded and wasted no time. That wasn't her way. "You aren't married, and am I right in the fact that you are sick of women throwing themselves at you, desperate for your money and the attention attached to their name if they were to land you?"

"You would be correct," Andrew said.

"I'm tired of the same. You know what I want, Andrew. To travel. You also know that as an unmarried woman, that's difficult."

"I'm not marrying you, Rosalee. We already agreed that we were friends. Nothing more."

"Which is all our marriage need be. One of convenience. We each get something out of it. To be left alone. You know I understand you. You understand me. We are two of a kind, Andrew." Rosalee gave him a sad smile. "This is the best we can hope for. A marriage of an agreement. Neither of us is getting younger, and while that's not an issue for you, as you are a man, it is for me."

He sighed. Rosalee was right. Except for one thing. A marriage of convenience wasn't what he wanted. He hoped still to have love. Knowing Evie had made him feel like there was the smallest of chances he could still have it. Saying yes to Rosalee would remove that. Even though the chance was remote...from the moment he'd met Evie, that tiny spark of hope had remained lit.

Rosalee was searching his face. "It's no, isn't it? You've got someone you like."

"Not at all," Andrew said quickly.

She laughed, and rested her hand on his cheek. "You might be able to lie to yourself, but you can't lie to me. We've known each other too long. So, who is she?"

He shook his head and stepped back from her grasp. "There's no one," he said.

"If you say so," Rosalee said. She leaned close and kissed his cheek. "Let's go in for dinner."

"If it's all the same to you," Andrew said, "I'd rather not."

Rosalee studied him carefully, then nodded. "Very well. Andrew, before you go, one thing."

"What's that?" he asked.

"Invite me to your wedding."

"There won't be one," Andrew said. Lowering his head a moment, he came as close as he would ever come to admitting what had happened. He gave a bitter laugh as he met her eyes and saw the sympathy in them. "I've messed things up in a way you wouldn't believe, and when the truth comes out, I'll be alone. I know it."

"Then she's not the one for you," Rosalee said. "But I hope you're wrong. One of us deserves to be happy."

He didn't miss the sadness in her eyes, nor in her voice. Andrew lifted one corner of his lips in a half smile, kissed her hand, and answered. "Yes, you do. Good evening, Rosalee. Enjoy the party. Don't hate me for saying no."

"I don't," she assured him, and this time her smile met her eyes. "It was just an idea."

An idea, he thought to himself on the way back home, that perhaps he should have considered except for two things. The first being he didn't want to be trapped in that lifestyle. One of all pretentiousness. Fancy meals, fancy dress, fancy manners. He wanted to get his hands dirty, not hire folks to do everything for him.

And then there was Evie. He hadn't meant to, but he'd been comparing every woman he'd seen as of late to her. Comparing their ways, their smiles, or laughter. Maybe Rosalee was right, and he was in love with her.

But he'd done something foolish, and it was too late to fix things. He'd not been wrong in that thought. Not one bit. He either needed to walk away before it was too late or else simply enjoy the time he had with her until she found out. Neither choice appealed to him. The thing was, he sensed that, like himself, Evie wasn't the sort of person to like a liar.

And that's just who he'd turned himself into.

Chapter 9

"The cornstarch, Evie, not the baking powder," Cook said, shaking her head.

"I'm sorry," Evie said, and reached for the correct jar. There was no reason to have gotten them mixed up, as they were clearly labeled. She tried to swallow down her embarrassment, but her cheeks still burned.

Cook didn't answer as she stirred and mixed, managing multiple pots on the stove as well as a bowl of dough behind her. "Go get me a half dozen apples."

"Yes, of course," Evie said, then hurried to the pantry. She opened the door and stood blankly as the rows of jars, sacks, and boxes faced her. Her mind was suddenly blank. What was it that Cook had wanted? She bit her lip as she let her gaze roam, hoping something would jostle her memory. Evie didn't want to go back and ask, but she couldn't remember what it was.

"Apples!" Cook shouted. "In the sack near the potatoes."

"I'm just getting them," Evie called back as she grabbed a half dozen. Once she hurried them back over to the kitchen, she washed them and set them on the counter.

"Is everything going well?" Mrs. Staunton asked as she walked into the kitchen. "It smells good."

"No thanks to Miss Head in the Clouds," Cook said, fixing Evie with a look. Then, she apologized, "Sorry, missy. You aren't usually like that. Not having a good day, are you?"

Evie's lip trembled, and she turned away, hoping to hide it. However, the astute Mrs. Staunton noticed, and rested a hand on her shoulder.

"Cook, will you be fine if I borrow Evie for a little?" Mrs. Staunton asked.

"Yes, ma'am," Cook answered.

"Come," Mrs. Staunton said. "Let's have tea in my office."

She quickly filled a kettle, put two teacups, saucers, a pot of cream, and a small bowl of sugar on a tray, and then nodded for Evie to carry it.

Evie followed the housekeeper out of the kitchen, down a hallway, and to the door of Mrs. Staunton's study. She didn't sense the housekeeper was upset with her, but stayed quiet, uncertain what to expect.

Mrs. Staunton opened the door and Evie followed her inside, then set the tray where indicated, on a small round table between two chairs.

Evie's eyes quickly glanced around the cozy room. She'd never been inside until now. There was a small fireplace and a screen in front. A good-sized window had dark green drapes over it, drawn back to let in the sunshine. There was a modest desk with a straight-backed chair before it, and of course the small setting here of two plush chairs and a table.

A few landscape paintings were on the walls, and a shelf with several books. Mrs. Staunton's knitting sat upon it, completing the study's decorations.

"Sit," Mrs. Staunton said, pouring the tea. She handed Evie a cup and poured for herself. She fixed her kindly gaze upon Evie. "Now then, tell me what has you so distracted."

"I don't mean to be," Evie apologized.

"I know that, dear," Mrs. Staunton said. Her expression was thoughtful. "I think I know you well enough now, after the time you've been here, to know that something must be wrong."

"It's my uncle," Evie said, her stomach churning at the memory. "I got a letter from him yesterday, and it wasn't filled with good news. He talks about how worrying things are for him just now."

She stopped and relaxed her hands on the teacup. Taking a deep breath, she continued, "He mentioned," and she lowered her voice, "that two men had come to his shop and harassed him. They demanded he make a payment larger than he'd expected."

"My goodness," Mrs. Staunton said, her voice low but alarmed. "What happened?"

"They roughed him up, and said they'd be back." Evie took a shuddering breath. "What am I to do?" Her troubled eyes met Mrs. Staunton's. "I send every bit of my pay. I cannot do more than that, and yet I must do more to help him! He needs me, and has spent his whole life looking out for me. I simply must help in some way. I just don't know what more I can do."

Evie's concern was reflected in Mrs. Staunton's expression. "My dear, I'm sure your uncle knows you are doing all you can to aid him. Might I add, more than most would? However, something you say concerns me a great deal. If you are sending him your all, what will you do when your dresses or shoes wear out? When you need something for yourself?"

Evie shook her head. "That doesn't matter to me. My uncle, and helping him, does."

Mrs. Staunton tsked. "You are employed at a reputable house of a wealthy rancher. You cannot look like a neglected housemaid. What would that say about Mr. Radcliffe? It's the furthest thing from the truth, but you know how people talk and tongues wag. How you act and how you look is a reflection upon this household."

Evie slumped in her chair. "You are quite right. I didn't think about that. Mr. Radcliffe, though I've not even met him, has been nothing but generous in his pay, and with my room and meals included."

Mrs. Staunton brightened. "Perhaps that's it, my dear. Why don't you speak with Mr. Radcliffe?"

"What do you mean?" Evie asked.

"Tell him what's happening. Perhaps he can help in some way."

Mrs. Staunton looked pleased at her idea, but Evie felt doubtful. The man had more to worry about than a housemaid's uncle.

Mrs. Staunton continued. "He is a good and generous man. Why, just a year ago, he paid for me to travel to be with my mother when she was gravely ill. I credit her recovery to the fact he got me there so swiftly."

"That is generous," Evie murmured. "I don't know." She looked down into her tea for a moment, then up at Mrs. Staunton. "But I will think on it."

"You do that," Mrs. Staunton said. "Now, go help Cook to plate the meal. Mr. Radcliffe won't be here for dinner tonight, so the three of us will dine together in the kitchen."

"Yes, ma'am," Evie said. "Would you like me to clear the tea away?"

"I'll do it," Mrs. Staunton said.

Evie nodded and left the study. As she hurried toward the kitchen, she didn't doubt Mrs. Staunton's sincerity that Mr. Radcliffe would help her if she asked, but how could she? She'd not really been there long enough to make a request of that magnitude. And what if he did offer her aid in some way, only her uncle wanted more and more? A strange feeling had come over her in the last letter or two, a sense that no matter what she sent, it would never be enough.

A deep sigh escaped, and Evie paused before the kitchen door. A heavy weight felt as though it were about to crush her. She'd hoped that talking with Mrs. Staunton would make her feel better, but it didn't.

Andrew. Perhaps Andrew might have a suggestion for her? She wasn't sure when she'd see him next. They passed each other occasionally near the house when she was out-of-doors running an errand for Mrs. Staunton, but they'd not had time to do more than wave or call out hello.

Still, she considered him a friend. Wasn't that what friends did? Asked each other for advice? At the moment, she wasn't sure who was taking advantage of who. Her uncle and the men at his shop, or her uncle and her. Regardless, she was in a situation she didn't enjoy and wanted out of. All she wanted was to aid her uncle and be done with it, so she could resume building herself a nest egg.

After all, housemaids rarely married, and though Spring Falls was a lovely town, there weren't many unmarried men in it, as many of them had sent for mail-order brides.

That might be her fate if she couldn't find a husband one day. Who knew where she'd be then? Evie shuddered. There was nothing wrong with becoming a mail-order bride. Some couples even found love, but she just couldn't fathom doing that. Leaving behind everything and everyone she knew, just for a chance at stability? What she wanted was love.

She pushed open the door to the kitchen and nodded as Cook bid her fill the water pitcher.

While she was outside at the pump, Andrew was walking toward the stable, Joe next to him. Andrew waved at her, and a little of the suffocating weight seemed to lift. It was funny how just a glimpse of him brightened her day.

Chapter 10

Rosalee's offer continued to float in Andrew's mind. He didn't know why, as he wasn't the least interested in her or a marriage of convenience. Was it that he was worried he was growing older, and a chance at a relationship had passed him?

Perhaps that crushing weight of loneliness was getting to him. It didn't matter how used to it he was, there were some times it got to him, brought him down. He'd been feeling that way as he'd walked toward the barn to leave for Rosalee's party. When he'd spotted Evie and they'd waved, it had eased, but only for a time. That one glimpse hadn't been enough, and the feeling hadn't dissipated, though the party had.

He knew he wanted more than just a casual relationship. He wanted a friendship and a partner in life—someone he could enjoy things with, but also a woman who understood he'd need to be busy with work at times, and he couldn't just traipse around the world, traveling or amusing her.

Evie wouldn't be like that.

The thought surprised him. Where had that come from?

There was a soft knock at his study door. "Enter," he called.

Mrs. Staunton walked in, holding a stack of letters. "The mail has arrived," she told him.

He looked at the thick bundle and inwardly cringed. Hopefully, it wouldn't be anything too disquieting. He'd been negotiating the sales of a dozen horses, and another hundred acres nearby. It was looking more likely those deals would be finalized, but both gentlemen he hoped to buy from were still not in agreement with the terms.

"Thank you," he said, taking the mail and setting it on his desk. He studied his housekeeper for a moment. "I meant to ask you, is all still going well with the household staff? Anything I should know about?"

Mrs. Staunton grew a thoughtful look. "I think everything is going well. The new housemaid continues to work hard. However, she's been a little distracted the last day or two. Hopefully that will change."

"Oh? Anything I need to be aware of?" Andrew asked. Why had Evie been distracted? Was something wrong?

"It's her uncle," Mrs. Staunton said, and her lips pressed together. "After several letters that seemed to distress her, he came into town, and she went to meet with him this afternoon. I admit, the man makes me uncomfortable. He came around and looked at the house before he picked up Evie. Perhaps it's nothing, but I got a bad feeling about him."

"Is that so?" Andrew asked. He frowned. "Any particular thing come to mind?"

"No, I can't put my finger on it," Mrs. Staunton said. "That irritates me greatly. I've had no such reservations about the girl. Perhaps it's that I know her uncle has been pressing her for money, and I don't like the way the man seems to be laying guilt on her."

"I see. Let me know if you see him again. I'd like to see what sort of a man he is myself," Andrew told her. "Perhaps I'll send word to town and ask Sheriff Steele if he'll keep an eye on things.

"I will let you know," Mrs. Staunton promised. "And that's a good idea. Asher Steele is a fine man. I've liked him from the moment he became sheriff. I did suggest she come talk to you. Explain the matter and see if you had any suggestions for her."

"Ah. Well, she has not," Andrew said, feeling himself tense. Was Evie planning to see him? And by him, he meant Mr. Radcliffe. How would he pull that off?

"She may not," Mrs. Staunton said. "She didn't seem to like the idea."

He nodded. Truth be told, he didn't like the idea either. It wasn't that he wouldn't help Evie. He would in a heartbeat. No, that just meant she'd see him. The real him. He wasn't ready for that.

"I'll leave now," Mrs. Staunton said. "Unless you've need of anything else?"

"Actually, yes. One more thing," Andrew said, remembering his concern from earlier. "I realize that you and the others work very hard. I am also aware that I do not know the half of what goes into running a household. If you need more help, be sure you have it. You have my permission to hire another housemaid or two if you need," Andrew said.

"Thank you, that is greatly appreciated," Mrs. Staunton said.

"One moment, before you go," Andrew said, and hastily penned a note to the sheriff.

If Mrs. Staunton was feeling concerned, he was as well. Perhaps all was well, and Evie wasn't being threatened or pressed to do something, but perhaps not. It wouldn't hurt to have the sheriff look into matters. After all, that's what he was there for.

"Can you get someone to send this to town?" he asked.

She glanced at the envelope and nodded. "Immediately," she said. "Thank you. It's a good idea. And thank you also for the offer of extra help. I might take you up on that." She left with her face beaming.

Good. He hoped that she'd consider what he said. He didn't want his employees to feel they were doing more than they should.

He went back to work, and a few moments later, once the mail was sorted, realized he was missing one of his reference books. Before he bid higher on the future foals of a breeder's stock, he wanted to be sure he was getting what he thought.

"Where did that go?" he wondered. He spent over a half hour digging through his study before he remembered he'd last had it in the sitting room, where he'd carried it in while he was looking for something else.

"I must have left it there," Andrew mused. "I'm becoming absent-minded. I wonder why."

He opened the study door and strode to the sitting room. He glanced around. It wasn't lying on a table, so perhaps the bookshelf. It was possible Mrs. Staunton or even Evie had seen it and put it there, not knowing any better.

Evie.

As usual, as soon as his thoughts landed on her, he grew contemplative. A small smile formed on his lips as he imagined her. What was she doing right now? Then, unease came over him. Mrs. Staunton said she was meeting with her uncle. How was that going? He was glad he'd sent a note to the sheriff.

Mrs. Staunton was an excellent judge of character, so for her to be concerned about the uncle made him feel that way as well. In truth, he knew that his curiosity and worry over Evie's wellbeing wasn't exactly because he was her employer. It was because he liked her.

In what capacity beyond friendship he wasn't sure, but he knew that something was growing between them, and he wasn't opposed to it.

But, like always, his lie was right there. The unwelcome visitor in the room. A small part of him hoped Evie would understand when the truth came out, as it was sure to do. But a larger part of him was scared of her reaction.

He sighed heavily. Never in his life had he worried about what another woman thought of him. There was no denying it. To him, Evie was more than just another human. She was a friend and so easily could be more.

Andrew scanned the titles on the bookcase for several moments before he found his book. Without wanting to wait, he opened it and searched through the pages until he found what he was looking for.

As he read, someone came into the sitting room, and he was surprised to see it was Evie. She held a duster in one hand. Her face was pale, and her eyes red, as though she had been crying.

Worry twisted into him. What had happened? Though he knew it was an irrational feeling, anger filled him at the idea her uncle might be taking advantage of her in some way. He tried to quell the thought. He knew nothing about the man. Knew little about her situation, but something made him want to rush to her, to comfort her, to tell her he could help in some way.

Help was something he could give. He had the money, the means, the reach. If necessary, he could do most anything. But how could he find out? How could he ask her what was wrong?

She seemed to sense him studying her, and turned just then. Her eyes were wide, but her face brightened slightly.

Andrew couldn't help it. A silly grin seemed to form as he walked closer. "Hello."

"Hello," she said, her voice soft, almost breathless. A smile stretched on her face. "It's good to see you," she told him. "I was hoping I would soon."

The words sent an electric current through his core. In what way did she mean that? He wanted to find out, but didn't want to presume. His eyes lingered over her sweet face, and on her tear-stained cheeks. Without even thinking, he reached out and stroked one.

Chapter 11

Evie flushed pink, and she was almost scared to breathe. She knew for a fact she didn't want to move out of reach of Andrew and his gentle touch. He was looking at her with such concern in his eyes, there was nothing more that she wanted to do than to unburden her soul of all that had happened the last few months.

Especially after today. Two letters weighed heavily in her pocket. She'd not returned to her room when she came back from seeing her uncle. There was his letter, which she'd gotten yesterday, telling of his newest worries, how he'd not even eaten for days, and the other. From a person who accused him of lying, and warned her of the danger she was in.

Seeing Andrew right now was such a blessing, she could hardly believe it. Then, she jolted. What was Andrew doing in the sitting room? She'd never seen any of the ranch hands here.

Confusion filled her voice, temporarily overcoming her recent upset, as she mentioned, "I've never seen you inside the house before."

"Ah. Yes," Andrew said, and his hand dropped from her face. He held up the book. "I was looking for this."

He looked slightly uncomfortable. Evie wondered why that was. "I'm glad you found it," was all she said. Then, she added, "It's nice you are allowed to borrow books. Do you enjoy reading?"

"I do," he answered, then he held up the book, "though this isn't for leisure. It talks about horses, and things to look for in regards to a breed I'm not too familiar with."

"Oh, I see!" she said, and nodded. "That's helpful. I've learned a good number of things from books."

"I have too," he said.

Her eyes traveled to the shelf of hardback volumes. "I wonder if Mr. Radcliffe would mind if I read some of his."

"You can—" he broke off suddenly, then continued, "You can ask Mrs. Staunton, I'm sure."

Evie shook her head. "I think she'd ask me to go ask Mr. Radcliffe. She suggested I do that recently for something else."

"Why didn't you?" Andrew asked.

She tilted her head. "What makes you think I didn't?"

He seemed a little flustered, but answered, "I just assumed you didn't, based on your apprehension to ask about borrowing a book."

She laughed at how he had noticed. "You are correct. I've still not met Mr. Radcliffe yet, but I've heard things about him, and hope they aren't true."

"What sorts of things?" he asked.

Evie hesitated. "I'm not trying to gossip," she said slowly.

"I understand that," he assured her. "But perhaps I can set your mind at ease."

"Oh! Perhaps you can," Evie agreed. "I've heard that he's demanding. Cold."

Andrew shook his head and shrugged. "Nah. I've heard others say that too, but it's not the truth."

"What is, then?" Evie asked curiously.

"He's a man who tries to treat people fairly, but when others try and take advantage of him, well, he has to be that way." Andrew was quiet a moment, then continued, "When a man has a lot of money, sometimes people think they are owed something. They just see he has, and thinks they should as well. They don't care that it was hard work, and still is hard work, that keeps a person there. That they do important things to help others, but not for those who have their hands out to try and trick them into something. That is why he values honesty and loyalty."

Evie felt tears come to her eyes unexpectedly, ones of absolute sadness and anger. His response hit too close to her recent meeting with her uncle. "I feel bad for him, then. It's difficult to feel like you are taken advantage of. Almost as though you don't know who you can truly trust or turn to if you need someone."

"Exactly," Andrew said. He met her eyes and seemed to be searching them. "I don't think you are that way at all."

She flushed and looked down. Their fingers were close, very close. Andrew moved the hand not holding the book and brushed it against hers. Without thinking, she curled her fingers around his, and their fingers entwined. There was a heavy silence, one that was filled with the need to say something. To move closer.

Andrew whispered, "Evie, if you ever need me for anything, anything at all, I'm here. However I can help, I will."

The words comforted her. He gently freed his hand and let it slide up her arm, to her elbow. Evie enjoyed the tingles over each inch he touched. She didn't want the moment to end.

"Promise me," he said, his eyes locked onto hers. "If you need help, in any way, you will come to me?"

Evie hesitated, and then she nodded. She felt torn. It was obvious they were attracted to each other. Likely, it couldn't go far, but would her seeking his advice take that away from her? In the last few moments, though her friend was standing before her, she sensed that there could be more. Wanted there to be more. It seemed that he might be feeling that as well.

"May I ask you a question, then?"

He nodded, but didn't move his hand. She was glad of that.

"Should we sit?" Andrew asked. He led her to one of the small sofas in the room.

"Oh! I'm not sure I'm allowed," Evie fretted. She bit her lip.

"It's fine," Andrew said. "If Mrs. Staunton comes in, I'll tell her I asked you to sit and talk with me for a moment."

She nodded slowly, still not sure, and a tiny voice in the back of her head wondered who he was that he was always so confident in the things he did, things that, usually, hired help wouldn't. Couldn't.

The thought left just as suddenly when his larger hands wrapped overtop of hers. "Tell me what's happened," he said, his voice quiet. "I can see you were crying, and I can tell something has upset you greatly."

Was it that obvious? Evie took a deep breath and nodded. She might as well tell him. She was in desperate need of advice. But what could she say without making anyone sound bad? Her uncle or herself.

Evie pursed her lips as she thought. Finally, gathering her thoughts as Andrew patiently waited, she asked, "If someone was taking advantage of another, what should they do?"

"It depends. In what way?" Andrew asked. There was something flickering in his eyes, something smoldering deep in his thoughts. She knew it wasn't directed toward her, but she shuddered anyway. It was too late now; she had to tell him.

Chapter 12

Andrew watched as a range of emotion flashed over Evie's face. He wanted to pull her into his arms, but the fact that they were in the sitting room alone, and she thought they weren't supposed to even sit on the sofa, kept him from doing so.

He saw sadness, hurt, and something akin to betrayal. It made him want to seek out who'd done this to her, and see they were properly removed from her life. Evie was looking at him, desperation in her eyes, yet she still hadn't spoken. He waited. He would wait as long as she needed. It was obvious whatever she was considering telling him was difficult for her.

Andrew let his thumbs stroke the backs of her hands, then gently squeezed. "I'm here. I won't judge. Only help, if I can."

She nodded, blew out a breath, and said, "You know I work to help my uncle. He raised me and is all I have, so I feel indebted to him."

"Of course you do," Andrew said quietly. He wasn't sure where she was going with this.

Evie withdrew her hands, though she looked reluctant at the action, and reached into her pocket, pulling out two envelopes. Andrew looked at them, then at her. "What are these?"

Tension in her voice, she told him, "The most recent from my uncle. It arrived yesterday. I...I met with him today. Mrs. Staunton let me go. The other also arrived yesterday. From a neighbor."

She handed him the first letter, and Andrew carefully unfolded it. A strong hand had penned the letter. It was short and to the point.

Got your money. Need more. I'm doing all I can to hold on to the place, but I'm running out of options. I've not eaten for two days. Everything goes toward the debt. I'm counting on you to come through for me. Who can you borrow from? Do what you must to get it. I have to have a thousand dollars by the end of the month.

Andrew was sure he looked as startled as he felt. Evie was looking at him, trembling now. "That is a good deal of money," he said slowly. "How and why does he expect you to get it for him? And what is this debt he speaks of?"

"I don't know," Evie whispered. "I never knew of one until recently."

A tear rolled down her cheek, and he brushed it away. His chest constricted at the conflicting emotions on her face. He wanted to help her. It was obvious to him now that Evie was being more than taken advantage of, and by someone related to her.

"He never told me how he accrued it. Nor an amount. And then...then there's this." She held out the other letter.

Andrew opened it. As before, he unfolded it slowly, afraid of what he might see. This handwriting was different. It was smaller, more precise, and appeared to be that of a woman. He read the words, and his heart sank. Slowly, he read them again.

Evelyn, I don't know how to tell you this, other than to speak plainly. Your uncle is a fraud. He's not losing his business. He's wasted his money, squandered it and every bit you've given him. He goes around bragging how you are an endless source and now work for a wealthy man and can get him whatever he wants.

Be careful. I am worried for you. He's no good and is taking advantage of you.

Andrew refolded the letter and handed it to Evie. "Who sent this?" he asked. "It isn't signed. Can you trust the sender?"

She nodded. "I recognize the handwriting. She's a woman of great standing. I do believe her. Today, when I met my uncle, it was because he came here to visit me."

"That's unusual," Andrew said, even though he'd already known the fact, having been told so by Mrs. Staunton.

"Yes. I knew it wasn't proper, and Mrs. Staunton gave me permission to spend an hour with him, off your property. We drove to town and back. The entire time, it was one tale after another about how he was in danger, how people were after him for his debt."

She bit her lip. "He pressed me to send him as much as I could. Thought I'd not given him all I have. I told him I had, and it didn't seem to satisfy him. If I had more to give, I would, but I don't even own jewelry. I have nothing of value. That's why I moved here to Spring Falls. I wanted to get a job. Save for my future.

"My uncle was angry. He raised his voice at me. Accused me of being selfish, of abandoning him. I don't know how long we talked. At last, he seemed to believe I had nothing more to give, and left."

"I'm sorry," Andrew said. He stood and paced for a moment, hoping to release some of the energy inside of him. Once he left Evie, he'd send another notice to the sheriff. She could be in danger. He'd need to tell him about the note from the anonymous person as well.

Andrew hesitated, then said, "Evie, I don't care for your uncle. If what this second letter says is true, I am quite concerned for you."

"What should I do?" Evie asked. "Is my uncle truly in danger? Or is he simply being dishonest? I don't know what to think."

Andrew stopped pacing. "Let me look into this. Make inquiries. Find out if that's all true."

"That would be wonderful, but how will you do that? I didn't know that a ranch hand would be so well connected? There might be a cost as well, and I...I don't have anything."

He stopped himself from freezing and running his fingers through his hair. That's right. He was Andrew, the ranch hand. A man of simple means. He was not supposed to be rich or connected.

"I know a man who lives nearby," he answered, recalling that he did have one there. He also had the sheriff. Asher Steele was a man of principles and dedicated to protecting all within his town. He knew he wouldn't sleep until they'd gotten to the bottom of this. "I'll ask him if he knows anything, and implore him to be discreet."

Evie nodded slowly. "Would you? But only if it's no trouble."

"None at all," Andrew said. "When is your next half day? We should ride again. Perhaps I'll have news by then."

She smiled. "I'd love that. In three days."

"Then that is when we will meet next," Andrew said.

Evie nodded, her smile radiant. His heart felt happier, seeing her leave the room with her shoulders looking less weighed down.

He left, making his way to his study, when he saw Mrs. Staunton. "Might I have a word with you?" she asked, almost stiffly.

Andrew nodded and led her to his study. They walked in, and she shut the door. She looked upset. Her usually smiling face was red, and her hands were trembling, clenched at her sides.

"Mrs. Staunton," he said in worry. "Are you all right?"

"I am not, Mr. Radcliffe," she answered, her pinned curls wobbling, "because I think that you are playing some terrible trick on that young woman."

"What do you mean?" he asked, even as his stomach started to churn.

"I heard part of your conversation," Mrs. Staunton said stiffly, "and it seems to me that young woman doesn't know who you are. She thinks you, Mr. Radcliffe, are a ranch hand! I do not know what game you are playing at, but it isn't right. Not to her. That girl is going through enough with that wicked uncle of hers. She doesn't need heartache on top of it."

"It's not a game," Andrew said. He jammed his hand through his hair. "It started by accident. And it's grown. I didn't mean to. But now, she thinks I'm just...Andrew."

He paced a few steps away and then turned back. "I wanted to tell her. But part of me liked being just that. Andrew. Not someone rich and connected and able to give. Now, hearing about her uncle, it makes me both glad I've kept that secret, and terribly guilty."

The look on Mrs. Staunton's face softened, and she stepped up to him. "Forgive me for thinking you were playing her false," she said. "Though you are, in a way, I understand. Can't say as I like it, and I don't approve, but I understand. Especially as I've known you for so long, and known all you've gone through with every woman who crosses your path."

"What am I to do?" Andrew groaned, sinking down into a sofa. He dropped his head into his hands. "I've made a mess of things. After what I said about Mr. Radcliff placing importance on loyalty and honestly...she'll think I'm a hypocrite."

"That's of your own doing," Mrs. Staunton scolded. "Perhaps you'll lose her friendship, playing at being something you aren't."

He couldn't even reply, he was so upset. She was right. And she wasn't telling him that to be unkind.

The sofa cushion moved, and he glanced over as she sat. One of her wrinkled hands landed on his arm, and she said, "Or maybe you'll get what you deserve. A woman who truly loves you for yourself."

His throat was tight, and he couldn't answer, but he desperately hoped so. Even if that could never happen, he wished for it. Mrs. Staunton stood and sighed. "I'll pray for you. That's all I can do, other than to keep quiet. But I won't stand by and watch you hurt her, so you remember that. She's as good as they come, and she's just right for you, I think."

He must have looked surprised, because she grew a wide smile. "I've not seen you this happy for a long time." She opened the study door and said, "You've got to tell her. The sooner the better."

Then, she left, closing the door behind her, and Andrew was alone with the thoughts that tortured him.

How could he tell Evie who he was?

Chapter 13

After she set down the box full of jars Cook had asked her to fetch, Evie poured herself a mug of water. Cook had been making jelly all morning. While the kitchen smelled lovely, a blend of berries and mint and pepper jellies, she was hot and tired. She was also glad it was her half afternoon.

"Evie, there's a note for you," Mrs. Staunton said, handing her a scrap of paper.

She turned away, giving Evie her privacy, and eagerly, Evie unfolded it.

Horse ride and picnic?

It was impossible to stop the smile on her face.

"Afternoon plans?" Mrs. Staunton asked.

"Yes, one of the ranch hands, Andrew, has been giving me lessons on how to ride. He's going to do it today, again," Evie said. "He also suggested a picnic. Is there something I might be allowed to take?"

"Andrew, hmm?" Nodding briskly, Mrs. Staunton said, "Leave that to me. You freshen up and stop by the kitchen before you go."

"Yes, ma'am," Evie said. "Thank you."

She hurried to her room, washed up quickly, and put on a fresh dress. After she ran a brush through her hair, Evie returned to the kitchen, not wanting to miss much of her time off.

Mrs. Staunton and Cook surprised her with a large basket. A clean cloth was tucked overtop of it. "Oh my," Evie said. "Do you think it's all right to take this much?"

"I do," Mrs. Staunton said, and shooed her out the kitchen door. "Enjoy yourself, dear."

"Thank you," Evie called as she headed to the barn. Her steps were light as she hurried along, eager to see Andrew and spend the afternoon with him.

As she walked into the barn, she saw that Starlight was saddled, as was Ginger. "Hello," Evie said.

Andrew looked up and then grinned. That lock of hair fell into his eyes. "Hello," he said.

"Mrs. Staunton packed us a meal," Evie said, gesturing to the basket.

"Here, I'll put it on my horse so you can just focus on your reins," Andrew told her.

"Thank you," she said, glad to surrender the heavy basket. What had Mrs. Staunton put in there? The kindness surprised her. Mr. Radcliffe really wouldn't mind? Between the large basket Mrs. Staunton insisted was fine, and the man's generosity in allowing her around his horses, Evie had almost made up her mind that he was a kind man. It was obvious to her that the others back at the boarding house had to have been mistaken.

Andrew helped her mount the horse. Evie's waist tingled where one of his hands rested as he stood beside her.

"Are you comfortable?" Andrew asked as he looked up at her. "I'll stand here as long as you need until you feel steady."

It was on the very tip of her tongue to lie, to ask him to stay there a moment longer, but she didn't dare be so bold. Her cheeks pinked at the very thought, but she answered, "I feel fine, thank you."

He nodded and mounted his own horse, then led them slowly in a walk out of the barn.

Evie tried not to clutch the reins, instead holding them the way Andrew had taught her, but she was a little nervous with him in front of her. What if something happened, and Starlight bolted? She hoped that the horse wouldn't, and also hoped that her nerves wouldn't make the horse skittish.

She forced her breathing to slow and be calm. Andrew had told her the horses would pick up on fear, to remain confident and not fearful. Luckily, as they rode out to a far pasture, she relaxed. Soon, she was enjoying herself.

"Here we are," Andrew said about fifteen minutes later.

He jumped down easily, then helped her. Again, his arms were around her, and she didn't miss how his hands lingered around her waist again, and his face was close to hers.

Had Starlight not walked forward, bumping her slightly and pulling them apart, Evie was sure she'd happily stay there forever.

Andrew grabbed the basket. "I've got a blanket. Want to eat now or in a little?"

"How about now?" Evie asked.

"That sounds good," Andrew said. He pulled out a blue blanket and shook it before laying it on a patch of grass.

Evie kneeled down and removed the covering on the basket.

"Mm! What have we got here?" Andrew asked.

She reached into the basket. "Looks like a loaf of fresh bread, some jam that we just made this morning, slices of ham, apples, cheese, pickles, and small savory pies," Evie announced.

Andrew's stomach grumbled loudly, and they both laughed, then helped themselves. As the two of them munched quietly, Evie couldn't help but feel content and relaxed. Something she'd not felt for a while. Some clouds had formed lazily in the sky, a few darker than others, but she hoped the weather held. She wanted to enjoy every moment with Andrew.

"I want to know more about you," Andrew said as he offered her a wedge of cheese, then stretched out, propping himself on an elbow. "What is it you want out of life? You seem so content right now, but have you any dreams or thoughts about what you'll do once you help your uncle?"

"I have, actually," Evie admitted. She reached for the ham and put a piece on her bread. "I just don't quite know how I'll make it work."

"Go on," he encouraged.

Evie glanced at him. He was giving her his full attention, as though what she had to say was important to him. It was a nice feeling, and something she'd never had until now.

"Well," she began, "I've always longed to help others less fortunate. Perhaps open a home for orphans, as I was almost one. Honestly, I suppose I am one, though I have my uncle. It's terrible to feel like you don't have anyone to love you when you are a child. It's even worse feeling like you don't know where you come from. There's a sense of loss. I want to prevent that for others."

His eyes filled with concern. "I admit, that's not something I have ever experienced, but I can see where that would be painful."

"It's that you just don't know your place," Evie said. "Where you fit in. You also wonder if you did something wrong. If the reason you are parentless could have been prevented in some way. It's hard to feel alone."

Her voice cracked at the last word, and an unexpected tear rolled down her cheek. Andrew sat up quickly and wiped it away. She liked the feel of his work-rough hand on her face. "You aren't alone," he told her. "You've got me."

"And I'm glad of it," Evie told him. "You've been a great comfort to me. I am...used to being lonely. It doesn't mean I like it, but I am used to it. I grew up that way, and I expect it's the same for most everyone else who had no real family. If you are used to something, even if it's a terrible or difficult thing, then it is easier to bear it. But I don't want others to feel that way."

"You're an amazing person," Andrew said. "I think you're going to do so much one day, Evie. You'll help so many people. Give so much love. I can tell you care deeply. The world needs more people like you." She blushed. His words were so unexpected, and he didn't make her feel like a fool—a housemaid becoming well off enough to support an orphanage. Most anyone else would have likely laughed, but not him. And she was so grateful for it.

"I've got to tell you something," Andrew said, almost reluctantly, as he reached for an apple.

"What's that?" Evie asked.

"I've not heard yet from either of my friends who were keeping an ear out for word about your uncle. I dislike potentially ruining the mood of our afternoon, but your words just now reminded me. I wanted you to know I'd not forgotten, and I had sent an inquiry. Two, actually."

Evie nodded and suppressed a sigh. "I appreciate it. Even if you don't learn anything, I am grateful to you for taking me seriously and trying to help."

"I'd do anything for you, Evie," Andrew said. That lock of hair fell in his eyes and he pushed it back, though he never broke the gaze they shared. "You are important to me. I want to help you if I can. Come to me whenever you need me. I will always be there."

Warmth filled Evie, and she glanced down in her lap. "Thank you," she said softly. "No one has ever said anything like that to me before."

He was quiet, almost as if he were wrestling with wanting to say something. Finally, he just moved a little closer and took her hands into his. "I mean it. My whole life, I've never had someone I could talk to the way that I can you. Almost every woman I've ever met doesn't see me for myself. They see me as a means to an end."

He swallowed hard and gave a small, bitter laugh. "It's not a good feeling."

Evie took one of her hands and brought it up gently on his arm. "I'm sorry," she said softly. "Perhaps it was because you are...too."

"Too?" he asked, his brow furrowed.

"Yes. Too. I know it sounds silly," she laughed and shook her head, "but it's the only word that works for you. Too. Too wonderful. Too kind. Too thoughtful."

"So, I should be less of those things?" he teased. "I should be cranky, and stingy, and selfish?"

Evie smacked his arm. "Of course not," she giggled. "But perhaps you are simply *too,* and that's the problem. They just want that." She reached for her bread and jam.

"Well, they can't have it," Andrew said. "I'm reserving all of it for you."

Evie's breath caught, and she was almost scared to look up at his face. When she set her bread down and dared look at him, all of the teasing and laughter was gone. Instead, there was something deeper. Hopeful. His eyes nearly burned through her as he stared at her.

Andrew took her hands in his again, and Evie found herself unable to breathe. Every inch of her was tense in anticipation of the words she hoped he would say.

His voice was soft, his gaze honest and open as he whispered, "Evie, I'm not sure just when it happened, but I'm falling in love with you."

Chapter 14

Andrew could hardly believe the words had slipped from his lips. Evie's face bore an expression of surprise, but her cheeks were that delightful rosy color whenever he said something that pleased her.

Internally, his heart was cracking. What she'd said about being used to loneliness...it was something he felt himself. Her words could have come from his lips. Goodness knows he'd thought the same many times.

The connection he was feeling with her only grew. It scared him in a way. He'd never felt like this, but he knew he'd done something foolish, and might have ruined his chance at the woman who seemed meant for him.

"Evie—"

BOOM!

The thunder jolted them, a split second after the first flash of lightning, and judging by the way they both lost their balance, Andrew knew there must have been a lightning strike nearby. Both horses made sounds of fright and ran from where they had been grazing.

"Oh no!" Evie gasped as she looked at their backsides streaking toward the barn. "What do we do?"

"They've run toward home," Andrew said, "and we will do the same. Let's get you back to the house before it—"

But he didn't have a chance to finish before the skies opened, and rain poured on them. Andrew had never seen anything so ferocious. Though it was going to be of little help, he still swept the remnants of their lunch into the basket and wrapped the blanket around Evie.

He took hold of her arm, and together they walked into the sudden wind. Each step forward was far more difficult than it should have been, and more than once Andrew looked with concern at Evie.

"I'm okay." She smiled at him, even though she likely didn't feel like the gesture.

The rain was cold, drenching, and Andrew hoped they'd get back the nearly two miles to the house before one of them caught sick.

All around them, trees swayed, some nearly bent in half, and the rain assaulted them from all sides. They took turns slipping in the freshly formed mud, and the next time that Andrew looked at Evie, her teeth were chattering. The rain had soaked them both, and he was sure his hair was as plastered to his face as hers was.

The house was within view, but the barn was closer. For a half second, he debated seeking shelter there, but as soon as he saw how weak Evie looked, he knew he had to get her to the house and dried off. The rain, still pounding, had caused a trench in the pathway, and water flowed. Evie slipped again, presumably on a slippery patch, and Andrew swept her into his arms. He was shocked to see he still held Mrs. Staunton's basket. They were so close now, there was no point in dropping it.

"I... can...manage," Evie gasped between her chattering teeth. Still, she clung to him, her arms around his neck.

"Shh, almost there," Andrew said, praying they'd make it soon.

To his great surprise, as soon as the house was only a few feet away, the door to the kitchen flung open. A surge of strength filled him, and he forced it into his legs, carrying them quicker. As he carried Evie into the kitchen, Mrs. Staunton and Cook's worried faces greeted him.

"My word," Mrs. Staunton fretted. "I'd hoped you found shelter."

"We did not," Andrew answered. "She was so cold, it would have been worse to stop at the barn and wait."

"I agree," Mrs. Staunton said briskly. She pulled away the sopping blanket, which just an hour before the two of them had lounged upon, and wrapped a large towel around Evie. "Let's go, my dear. Can you make it?"

"Y-y-yes," Evie chattered.

"Get yourself dry," Mrs. Staunton scolded Andrew with a backward glance as she hurried Evie out of the room.

That's just what he did, then returned to the kitchen. Cook served him a hot drink and steaming soup. Andrew wasn't sure he'd ever be warm again, but he was worried about Evie. How was she faring? He paced in the kitchen until Mrs. Staunton came in, then looked at her anxiously.

"I know what you are thinking," she said, holding up a hand. "And no, you may not go check on her. It wouldn't be appropriate. Especially considering the circumstances of who you are, *Andrew*."

He grimaced. She was right. This was just another way he'd made things more difficult for himself. So, he did all he could do in that moment. Took a breath to try and calm his racing heart, and asked, "How is she?"

"Dry now. Mostly stopped shivering. But we'll know more in the morning. I told her to stay in bed."

"I'll take her more tea soon," Cook offered. "Poor dear might catch sick."

"That's my worry," Mrs. Staunton agreed grimly. "That storm came from nowhere and was quite nasty."

"It's letting up," Cook said, "for all the good that it did."

"I expect to hear word about a lot of damage," Andrew said, shaking his head. "I hope there were no injuries. I'm going to go to my study. You'll...let me know if..."

"Yes. Now, out of my kitchen," Mrs. Staunton scolded.

Andrew hardly slept that night when he finally left his study. He was worried about Evie. When morning came, he put himself right into the kitchen again, even with Mrs. Staunton glaring at him. It didn't matter it was his house and his ranch. This was her kitchen, and she made sure he knew it.

"Are you going to sit here all day?" she asked immediately when she came in and saw him.

Cook wasn't around, so he answered, feeling a little awkward, "I reckon it's the only place in the house appropriate for a ranch hand to sit."

She nodded, giving a small smirk, but then she sighed. "I was coming to look for you anyway. Evie's got a fever, and her throat is inflamed. I've sent for Dr. Justin Davis. You know, that nice young doctor who moved to Spring Falls last year and married Charlotte Harrison? He should be here soon."

His chest constricted. He'd hardly heard what she said. His mind stuck on two words. Evie. Sick. And it was all his fault.

No, he knew it wasn't, not really, but that didn't make him feel any less responsible.

Andrew sat glumly in the kitchen, and jumped to his feet once the doctor arrived. They greeted each other, then he paced for what seemed to be a half hour before Dr. Davis came into the kitchen.

"How is she?" Andrew asked.

"Very ill," Dr. Davis answered, his tone serious. "But I think she will recover quickly if she stays in bed for a few days, drinks plenty of fluids, and takes the medicine I've left. The biggest concern, of course, is pneumonia. I've given Mrs. Staunton orders for poultices and hot bricks at her feet, lots of broth and tea."

"Thank you," Andrew said.

"If you need more help, send word, day or night. If I am with a patient, my wife, Charlotte, will come. She is a more than competent nurse, and can at least assess the situation until I can get here," he said.

Mrs. Staunton showed the doctor out and, momentarily alone, Andrew hesitated, then hurried toward the stairs. He climbed the two flights of steps as quickly and as quietly as he could. He knew he shouldn't be there, but he wanted to check on Evie.

When he peered through the crack in her door, her sweet pale face was on her pillow, her eyes closed. Andrew swallowed a lump in his throat and went back down the stairs.

He almost wished he hadn't seen how ill she looked. Now, the disturbing image would follow him. If she didn't recover, he didn't know what he'd do.

When he got down the stairs, Mrs. Staunton was standing there, hands on her hips. She didn't say a word, though, just looked at him sorrowfully. "She'll be fine," she assured, though there was hesitation in her voice.

"Take care of her," Andrew said, knowing that his tone was one of begging. "Please." He didn't even care how his voice had cracked on the request.

Mrs. Staunton nodded solemnly, squeezed his shoulder, and then pushed him toward his study. He went so that she wouldn't see the fear in his eyes.

It was there in his study, or Mrs. Staunton's kitchen, that Andrew spent the next four days. He knew he wouldn't be able to sleep, so did little more than doze on the sofa in his office before startling awake to check on any news of Evie.

During his time waiting, he worked on an idea, one that had sprung to his mind during one of his conversations with Evie. When she'd talked about being an orphan, and that loss she felt not knowing if anyone cared for her, it had shaken him. In fact, the thought hadn't left his mind.

What must that be like to a child? One of any age, to feel alone and uncertain of their place in the world. Without someone who cared for them to guide them or protect them, it would be very lonely. He could see where that was also the kind of circumstance that led to desperation, and desperation often led to serious or dangerous outcomes.

Although he knew he already did things for others, the thought came to him he could do more. Like giving those children a chance for their future. He remembered when he was a boy, all the hopes and dreams he had. In fact, right now he was living many of them, by owning this ranch. That wasn't something he could have done without the help and support of his own parents.

But what of a child who didn't have a family? Perhaps...he could be that person for them. The idea appealed to him, and filled him with such a sense of purpose, he'd begun forming an idea on how to do such a thing. He couldn't wait to tell Evie what it was.

In truth, it was the sole thing that kept him occupied, that kept complete worry from consuming him. Evie was so weak, he worried for her constantly.

In that time, two letters came from that no-good uncle of hers. To say he wasn't tempted to look was a lie. He was. Mrs. Staunton glared at them each time she walked past them sitting on the kitchen counter. Once, he was certain he'd heard her mutter something very unladylike. It made him smile—the first in days—because he felt just the same at the thought of Evie's uncle.

He'd heard from Sheriff Asher. So far, he and his deputy, Jeff, hadn't learned of any misdeeds. It simply might be the man was trying to take advantage of his niece, especially since he knew she was working for a wealthy man. Andrew desperately hoped that wasn't the case, but he planned to be ready at the first sign of trouble.

Sheriff Steele was as well, and Joe and Mrs. Staunton had been told to send right away for the sheriff—without delay—if the man showed up again. Both promised, and Joe had been lingering near the house more often, keeping an eye out.

A knock at the door made Andrew look up from his mug. Dr. Davis stood at the kitchen door. Cook let him in. At the same time, Andrew stood.

"I'm here to check on the patient," the doctor said. "She was a little improved yesterday, so I hope to see that continue into today's visit."

"I'll take you," Mrs. Staunton said from the doorway, and led the way out of the kitchen.

While she was gone, there was another knock at the back door. Joe stood, hat in his hands. When Andrew opened it, Joe said, "Just letting you know we got most of the cleanup done. We sure were lucky. No one and no livestock hurt."

"Thank you," Andrew said. "I should have been out helping."

"Nonsense. That's what you pay us for," Joe said. "How's the girl?"

"The doctor is with her now," Andrew answered.

Joe reached over and clapped his shoulder. "She's going to be fine. At least till she hears what you've been hiding. Then, it might be you needing the doctor."

It was impossible to not growl at the words, but Joe chuckled heartily at his joke and turned, leaving Andrew to sit back down and wait, something he'd become used to over the last few days. If only Evie did recover, he'd gladly take her anger. He deserved it. He just wanted her well. There was nothing else that mattered to him, and there never would be.

Soon, footsteps sounded on the stairs, and he stood as the doctor entered the room with Mrs. Staunton. "No fever," Dr. Davis said, looking cheerful. "Her throat looks much better, and her chest is still clear. Two more days in bed, and then light duties."

Andrew nodded. "Thank you," he said, then closed his eyes a moment in relief.

"Anytime at all," the doctor said, then let himself out.

Feeling as though now he could actually concentrate on work, Andrew walked to the doorway. "I'll be in my study," he said as he left the kitchen. He headed into the hallway, then changed his mind and hurried back up the two flights of steps.

Evie's door was cracked, and he peeked one eye through.

"Andrew?" her voice was weak, but there was no mistaking her smile.

He eased the door open and stepped inside. "I wanted to see for myself how you were," he admitted.

"You shouldn't risk getting in trouble or losing your job over me," she said, the worry evident in her face.

Andrew took her hands and pulled them to his lips to press a kiss on each palm. "You worry too much about me," he told her. "I don't care about any of that. I wanted to check on you. In case you hadn't noticed, I like you. And... once you are better, I need to tell you something important. I can't—shouldn't—wait any longer. I already have, much to my shame."

"What is it?" Evie whispered.

He debated telling her right now. Telling her that he was Mr. Radcliffe. But she was still weak. Would the shock be too much? It might be, and her health was still fragile. No, it was too much of a risk. He didn't even dare tell her what he'd been working on, and was close to doing. It might get her too worked up. Rest and recovery was what she needed.

"When you are better," he promised, pushing her hair away from her eyes.

"Very well," she said, leaning slightly into his hand, though she looked disappointed.

Andrew was about to say something when the sound of someone on the stairs sent him bolting out of the room and hiding in a shadow. As Mrs. Staunton walked past his hiding place and into Evie's room, he went down the stairs as swiftly as he could, then into his study.

Once there, he sat at his desk and dropped his head into his hands. Evie was always so worried about him. He'd never had anyone really care about him the way she did. Would she still, once she knew he was nothing but a liar?

Chapter 15

Andrew liked her! She hadn't been imagining he'd told her that, or that he was falling in love with her. Evie couldn't stop his words from singing in her mind. At first, she'd thought she'd dreamed his original confession, as she'd been fevered for a few days after getting caught in the terrible storm.

Joy at knowing he had truly said it, and had actually meant it, filled Evie with such happiness, she wanted to leap from her bed and go find him.

But, of course, she couldn't. Her legs were still a little weak, and she tired very quickly just moving from the bed to the chair. Dr. Davis had told her she could resume light duties in a few days, and Mrs. Staunton told her that's all she'd be doing—very light work.

While Mrs. Staunton was being very kind and thoughtful, showing her concern over her welfare, Evie was worried. First, how would she pay for the doctor's fees? Next, what would Mr. Radcliffe say? She was not working. And if she didn't work...panic suddenly filled Evie. If she didn't work, she wouldn't get paid. If she wasn't paid, then her uncle...

Distress filled her, and she struggled to get out of bed. Unfortunately, in her haste she became so tangled in the blankets that she fell to the floor with a thump. Mrs. Staunton burst into the room a moment later, as Evie was struggling to stand.

"What happened?" the housekeeper exclaimed as she assisted Evie up from the twisted pile of bedclothes.

"I was trying to get out of bed," Evie said. Then, she gave a small laugh. "I succeeded. Though not in the way I expected."

"You may sit in the chair," Mrs. Staunton scolded her. "But no wandering about."

"But I feel fine," Evie said, trying to give her brightest smile. "I'm quite able to return to work."

"The doctor says otherwise," Mrs. Staunton retorted as she straightened the blankets on Evie's bed, then wrapped one around her shoulders.

"But I must work," Evie said. There was no hiding her panic. "How else will I pay for the doctor? Or earn wages? I must send them to my uncle."

"Is that what this is about?" Mrs. Staunton asked, clucking her tongue. "Mr. Radcliffe has paid for the doctor. You also will get full wages."

"But...that's not right," Evie said, distressed. She worried her fingers around the blanket's edge. "He doesn't even know me. I've never met him. It...it doesn't seem right."

"There are a lot of things with Mr. Radcliffe just now that aren't right," the housekeeper said rather cryptically. "But, speaking of your uncle." She reached into her pocket and withdrew four letters.

Evie looked at them for a long moment, then finally reached out her hand to take the envelopes. She was scared to open them and see what he had to say.

"I think you should leave them," Mrs. Staunton said. "Wait a few days. Until you are better. Seeing them now might only upset you and make your recovery slower."

With a slow nod, Evie knew she agreed. But she had to read them. "Mrs. Staunton," she asked softly. "Might I go sit outside just for a little while? I am so tired of being in here."

There was a long pause, and then Mrs. Staunton nodded. "Yes. You may. In fact...wait here just a moment. I'll be right back."

Evie did as she was told. While she waited, she opened the letters in order of the date they were sent.

I have not heard from you for several days. I somehow made the payment, but have sold off everything in the house. I'm not sure what I'll do.

She bit her lip and reached for the second letter. As Evie skimmed it, then opened the third, she read much the same. Though this time, there was a tone of anger in the words.

The final note read, *Why have you not written or sent money? You'd leave me to suffer, after all I have done for you? Are you spending it all trying to impress that wealthy man you work for? Wasting it on dresses and frippery, while I starve? It's been rough here. I don't know why you've abandoned me, but I know you'll do the right thing. If you don't, I'll have to take matters into my own hands, and I won't go down alone.*

Evie slowly folded the letters. She had to write him back, but what would she say? She'd tell him she'd been sick, send the money...but a feeling inside her told her that would not be enough to satisfy him. What did he mean, he'd take matters into his own hands and wouldn't go down alone? Was that a threat that he'd engage in some sort of lawlessness?

A moment later, she was surprised to see Mrs. Staunton returning, Andrew right behind her with a wide grin on his face.

"Mr—Andrew, is going to help you down the stairs," the housekeeper said.

"Oh! I can manage," Evie assured, though now that she remembered the two flights of steps and the long hallway, she wasn't so sure.

"Nonsense," Mrs. Staunton said.

Andrew walked in and winked at her. Then, before she'd hardly realized it, had swooped her and the blanket into his arms and carried her from the room easily.

Evie hardly dared breathe as Andrew carried her down both flights of stairs, down the long hallway, and out through the kitchen door. He set her carefully on a bench, then sat next to her. "Are you comfortable?" he asked. "Should I get another blanket?"

"I feel wonderful, thank you," Evie said. "You didn't have to carry me."

"Oh, yes, I did!" Andrew said. "Mrs. Staunton told me to. Do you want to argue with her?"

Evie giggled. "Not really."

"Exactly. You understand, then." Andrew leaned back and crossed his arms. "I'm glad you are doing better. I was worried for a while." He stared at her critically, as if assessing for himself whether she was well.

"I feel almost normal," Evie told him, "except for getting tired easily."

"Fresh air will do you good," he told her. "I'm happy to carry you up and down the stairs as much as you need."

"I'm sure I'll be able to do it myself tomorrow," she said with a smile. "Besides, I have to get back to work. I don't want Mr. Radcliffe to think I'm lazy."

"That's the furthest thing from anyone's mind," Andrew said, leaning forward. He stared at her incredulously. "What makes you think such a thing?"

Evie shrugged. "I've not worked for a week. A household doesn't run itself."

"You rest," he told her firmly. "Stop worrying about your job, and what Mr. Radcliffe thinks. Mrs. Staunton has everything well in hand."

Andrew stared off into the distance, and Evie noticed his jaw clenching. She wondered why. It seemed she'd upset him, and she didn't want that. Shyly, she reached over and rested her hand on his arm. "May I ask you something?"

"Of course." His expression cleared instantly, and it made her wonder what he'd been thinking about.

"You told me you liked me," she said softly.

"I did. I mean, I do." Andrew's eyes blazed into hers. "I mean that with all of my heart. I also meant what I said, about how I was falling in love with you."

Her heart pounded. Andrew took her hand in his and gently squeezed it. "I guess I should know, though, how you feel about me. Do you feel the same?"

"I do," Evie breathed. "I like you, and I love you. I think that I have for a long time."

His eyes searched her face, and nervousness seemed to come into them. "So, you love me for who I am? Just...what I am? The person you know?"

"What a funny question," Evie said. She laughed and shook her head. "Of course I do. Why wouldn't I? In truth, I am not much of anything myself. I have nothing to offer anyone, so it amazes me that you care for me as I am."

"Don't say that." His tone was sharp. "I don't want to hear you speak poorly about yourself. Of all the women I've ever met, I know you are the most special. I know that my heart wants you, my soul wants you, and all of the love that I have to give is just for you. There's no one else. It wouldn't matter to me if you were wealthy or poor. Those things don't make a person. What does is who they are. And I see all that you are."

Evie blinked back tears. "Is that so?" she whispered.

He nodded. "Yes. You are...too." Andrew grinned then.

"Too?" Evie asked.

"Yes. Too kind, too sweet, too thoughtful and caring. Things I don't think anyone has ever been—not genuinely—to me."

"I'm sorry you've not had those things," Evie said, her voice serious, "but at the same time, I'm so glad that I've been able to give you that, and to know that as much as I love you, you love me too."

"I do," Andrew whispered. "Evie, I will love you forever. There is no one that I want but you." Then, he leaned in, and his lips met hers.

Chapter 16

Evie's sweet, soft mouth was pressed to his, but not for long enough. In fact, he'd hardly brushed her lips when the back door opened, and they startled apart. Evie's face was flushed, and she stared into her lap.

As for himself, Andrew glared at Mrs. Staunton, who looked flustered. He wondered if he was in for another scolding when he noticed her twisting her hands. She looked distracted. Upset.

"Evie," she said in a strange voice. "You...have a visitor."

"I do?" Evie stared at her in surprise, and then the color drained from her face. "It's my uncle, isn't it?"

"I'll send him away," Andrew growled, and stood.

But Evie's hand rested on his arm. "No, I must speak with him." She stood and asked, "Mrs. Staunton, might we use the sitting room? I-I don't think I wish to be alone with him."

"Of course," the housekeeper said.

Andrew closed his eyes as they went into the house. He was finally about to tell her. He was finally going to tell her who he was. That he was Mr. Radcliffe. That he'd not meant to, but he'd inadvertently let her think he was a ranch hand, and didn't bother to correct her. And that afterward, he didn't know how to tell her. How there never seemed to be a right time.

And of course, this was another one of those times that it didn't work out. How many would there be?

Frustration filled him. Yes, he could still tell her, but, once again, the moment seemed to have passed. Still, the important thing was that they loved each other. Love could overcome any obstacle, couldn't it?

Even...a lie?

Andrew walked into the house. "Mr. Radcliffe," Mrs. Staunton said quietly at the far edge of the hallway. "Joe's run for the sheriff. I am near if she needs me. She knows to shout for me."

He nodded in gratitude. She was a good woman. It also would be good to have Sheriff Steele, just in case. He went toward his study, intending to give Evie privacy, but paused when he heard her voice from the sitting room. He couldn't make out the words, but she sounded upset. Angry.

Hesitating, he drew closer to the sitting room, wanting to be there if she needed him. He had no qualms about putting her uncle out on his ear, and he'd gladly do it if that was what Evie wanted. In fact, he'd wait there. Perhaps he'd have the pleasure of doing so.

The conversation grew clearer to his ears as he stopped outside of the sitting room and crossed his arms, not even hiding to anyone passing by that he was listening. The door was closed, but he could be inside in a moment if Evie called out for help.

"And why not? You work for a wealthy man."

The man, obviously her uncle, was raising his voice. It was all Andrew could do not to burst in. He didn't like the man's tone, and he especially didn't like his words. How would Evie respond? He decided to go inside.

"Yes, Uncle, I do work for him. I work hard, and I'm proud of my hard work. That's why I won't do what you ask. I won't betray him."

Andrew froze, his hand on the door's knob. What had he missed?

"You aren't betraying anyone but your only family," her uncle said. "Selfish girl. Don't you care about me?"

"I...I do." Evie sounded conflicted. Hurt.

Andrew started to turn the knob, planning to put a stop to the turmoil that no-good man was putting her through, but her uncle's next words made his blood turn cold.

"Then do what I tell you. He's a rich man. He'll never notice. A few knickknacks here...a few there...I sell 'em. We could have a good thing going on. Heck, you said you've never even seen the man. Bet he's hardly around. There's no one to notice, and who'd believe a girl like you would do that? You can keep a third. Build yourself a little nest egg. Pursue your foolish dream of an orphanage. So, what do you say? Help your uncle out."

There was a roaring sound in Andrew's ears, and his hand fell from the knob. He stumbled down the hallway, only making it about a dozen steps before his legs gave out and he slid to the floor, the wall supporting his back.

Her uncle was telling her to steal from him. Had thrown out a bait she surely wouldn't be able to refuse—both guilt at helping him and the desire to help others. Who would turn that down?

He'd never felt so betrayed in his life.

Chapter 17

It had taken all of Evie's strength to stand instead of sit before her uncle. As he spoke, his words sounding more and more distressing to her ears, she wondered if she really knew him at all.

Yes, he'd taken care of her growing up. But...memories rushed back now of her always doing the caring. Of her cooking and cleaning or working in the shop, doing odd jobs, buying the food that she couldn't manage to grow.

From the earliest time she could remember, there had been neighbors clucking and shaking their heads. Dropping off a loaf of bread, a pie she was fortunate to get a slice of. A worn dress someone had outgrown and she taught herself to make fit.

Evie began to tremble. At first, she wasn't sure why. She wasn't cold. Perhaps it was because she was weak from being so ill? But her strength had returned for the most part. That couldn't be it.

Her uncle scowled, and the words that spewed from his lips horrified her. "Then do what I tell you. He's a rich man. He'll never notice. A few knickknacks here...a few there...I sell 'em. We could have a good thing going on. Heck, you said you've never even seen the man. Bet he's hardly around. There's no one to notice, and who'd believe a girl like you would do that? You can keep a third. Build yourself a little nest egg. Pursue your foolish dream of an orphanage. So, what do you say? Help your uncle out."

He grinned at her then, laughed, and waited for her to agree. That is when it struck Evie. She was shaking because she was angry.

She'd never felt such rage before. He was using her guilt for his wellbeing, and her dream of helping others, and throwing it back into her face. Even now, he stood before her, laughing, as though this were all one colossal joke.

Suddenly, a strange calm filled her, likely showed as well, but underneath her skin she was hotter than the blacksmith's forge, angrier than the storm that had opened up on her and Andrew.

In that moment, she knew what she'd have to do. And the price she'd have to pay. What she was about to tell her uncle was going to lose her the one thing she'd just gotten. The one bright spot in her life that had filled her with so much joy.

Andrew.

Her stomach felt sick.

"I'm waiting," he said. "Cat got your tongue?" He laughed, an ugly, cruel sound that made her feel sick.

"No, Uncle," Evie answered, surprised at the coldness in her tone. "I was waiting to hear if you were joking, as from your expression it had seemed so, but it appears that you are serious."

"Of course I am," he scoffed. "Now, give me your answer." He glanced about. "Perhaps those candlesticks. I can just take a few on my way out. Are they silver? Always take them in pairs," he told her, as though he were giving her a valuable lesson. "Missing just one makes it obvious. If two are gone, someone assumes they are stored somewhere."

"No." Evie stood as tall as she could and held a hand out in front of the candlestick that sat on the side table. "Just because you've made a mess of your life does not mean I intend to do the same with mine. That's my answer. I'll never do such a thing. How could you even ask me to? What kind of a person do you think I am, to betray another so easily?"

Her uncle's face was filled with fury. Had the sofa not been right behind her, Evie might have stepped back to widen their distance.

"Do you even know what you are saying? You worthless girl. You're going to betray me? After all I've done. You'll regret this. I'm giving you one last chance to change your mind." His voice was cold. Hard. Gone was any glimpse of the man that she thought she knew.

"No." Her voice, though wobbly, spoke her surety. "I won't regret it, but you will because now you won't get another thing from me."

Evie stepped forward. It wasn't much of a step, but she moved forward and bravery filled her. She was sacrificing her own happiness, and an ache filled her, but there was no way she was going to betray her friends. Mrs. Staunton, Cook, Andrew. Even Mr. Radcliffe, who she'd never met but who had been nothing but kind by proxy.

"You ask me to steal from those who have offered me a job and treat me well? I refuse to do it. You get nothing now. I will have nothing to give. You know as well as I do, word will get out what you asked me to do. I'll lose this job. I'll have no references, but I will have everyone whispering about me. No one will ever hire me. You took that from me. You've taken my future, and by way of that, your future too."

Her voice grew stronger. There was no wobbling now. Just determination to say what was in her mind and on her heart. What she should have said before. "For once, I felt like I had a place and an opportunity. I had such hopes I'd be able to set aside money for my future. Then, I got your letter. The moment I did, my thoughts were only of helping you. I see now that wasn't enough. Nothing ever was. You say I'm betraying you? You have betrayed me. It stops here. I will not—not today, not ever—be disloyal to those in this household, no matter the cost to myself. Go. I don't want to speak to you again." Evie raised her chin.

He looked at her a long moment, as if waiting in disbelief. Finally, he shrugged. "Fine by me," her uncle growled. "Works both ways, girl. Don't come running to me for anything. You'll need plenty because you got one thing right. You'll have no work. I'll be sure you lose this job, and any other you try to get. No need to wait for them to hear it from others what kind of a person you are. I'll tell them myself."

Evie didn't answer. In truth, she was scared she might cry if she opened her mouth. Pressing her lips together was the only way she could keep them from trembling.

Her uncle strode toward the door to the sitting room, then stopped, his hand on the knob. "I should have never even wasted my time with you. Know what's funny? You're not even family. I just called myself your uncle. You were the daughter of my friend. Should have known you were just as worthless as he was. Your mother was too. Weak. That's why she died giving birth. Then, your father took sick and followed her. I should have left you lying there next to them. Rid myself of the trouble. I was soft, but I won't make that mistake again. You're on your own. Back where you started. Alone."

He pulled open the door and left, filling the room with his heavy words that had changed everything. Breathing hard and feeling lightheaded, Evie stumbled from the room. She wasn't sure what to do now. Nothing had fully sunk in. She only knew she had to warn Mr. Radcliffe. Tell him she would quit, but he needed to protect his property. Perhaps send for the sheriff, if it wasn't too late.

She was terrified at the idea. She'd never met him before. And now...this would be his first and last impression of her. A hysterical woman who brought word of her relative out to steal from him.

No matter. She'd brought all of this to him, and she had to take responsibility and warn him. Evie choked back a sob and headed toward Mr. Radcliffe's study. Along the way, she prayed he wouldn't yell at her. She wasn't sure she could take much more of that.

To her surprise, Andrew was in the hallway. The expression on his face was one she couldn't quite decipher.

"Andrew," she said, rushing over to him.

"Evie." His tone was strange. Almost cold.

"I'm so glad to see you. I...I don't know what to do. But I must talk to someone." Evie twisted her hands together.

"Is it about your uncle? Asking you to steal something?" There was no mistaking it now. His tone was cold. "Do you intend to do what he asked?"

She looked at him in surprise. Had he heard some of their argument? Evie shook her head. "No. I told him to leave. That I wouldn't betray those I work with or work for. I told him I'd lose my job, as well, and he'll never get another thing from me. And I know I will, once I tell Mr. Radcliffe, but I have to tell him. If my uncle were to try to cause trouble..."

"Sheriff Steele and his deputy came," Andrew said. "He's been escorted off the property. He won't be welcome back. Not here, and not in Spring Falls."

Evie closed her eyes in relief. "I'm so glad. But at the same time, I don't know what I'll do. I have nothing and no one now." A sob forced its way out, and she said, almost hysterically, "Actually, I never have had anyone. He told me we aren't even related. I'm worthless and an orphan. But I refuse to bring trouble to a place that doesn't deserve it. I'm on my way to tell Mr. Radcliffe, beg his forgiveness for the trouble I caused, and then leave."

She took another step forward. Andrew grabbed her arm. "You're leaving?"

"Yes. It's the only way. Oh, Andrew. I'm so sorry. I can't think what else to do to protect everyone here, including you. As scared as I am to face Mr. Radcliffe, the thing that upsets me the most is that when I leave, I will lose you. I don't know where I'll end up, but I'm sure I can't stay in Spring Falls."

Andrew didn't say anything, though Evie could see a muscle working in his jaw.

He gritted out, "Don't you think this should be discussed first?"

"Discussed?" Evie shook her head. "What—"

Someone came into the hallway then. Mrs. Staunton. She took in the scene before her with a cool gaze. Then, much to Evie's surprise, she stood next to Evie, crossed her arms over her chest, and addressed Andrew. "Well. What a day full of shocking news this has been. What do you intend to do now?"

Chapter 18

Andrew stood there, his mind filled with indecision. He wasn't sure what to think right now, nor what to believe. When he first heard Evie's uncle's plan, he had hoped she would rebuke him. But though she claimed she had, he had been so shocked, he hadn't stayed to hear.

It was something he now regretted. How was he to know she was telling him the truth? He'd never met a woman who had. Even Evie, with all of her good intentions, might be just as selfish as the others when the time came for what she wanted, which appeared, right now, was to leave. Was that her thinking about herself? Or was she being truthful, that she wanted to protect him?

And now, to complicate things further, Mrs. Staunton, who knew his secret, stood there, waiting for him to say something.

Of course Evie was telling the truth. Wasn't she? Andrew dropped his hand from her arm and let his eyes examine her. She didn't look guilty. No, she looked upset. Worried. Earnest. She was speaking to Mrs. Staunton.

It was then he realized he must still be in shock, as he'd not even heard a word of what she'd been saying. He'd been so lost in his own thoughts.

"I must tell him," Evie said, her voice desperate. "Is he in his study? I hope Mr. Radcliffe won't hold my uncle's words against me. At least give me a reference? I'll leave willingly, I promise, perhaps go to Cottonwood Falls, but—"

"Shush," Mrs. Staunton interrupted Evie. She focused her attention on him again, her eyes asking, *Now what will you do?*

He still hadn't answered. Indecision still weighted him, as though it were a sack of stones on his back.

"There is no more waiting, no more delaying," Mrs. Staunton said to him.

Her voice was firm. Not angry, but filled with warning. He watched her, feeling almost numb. The moment was here. He had to choose.

She had wrapped an arm around Evie's shoulders. "You've made your bed. It's time to lie in it."

She walked off then, and Evie stared at her as the housekeeper strode further away. "I'd have thought her words were for me," she said as she turned to meet his eyes, "considering the situation. But she was talking to you. What...what did she mean?"

"She meant, I'm a liar," Andrew said. Disgust filled him. Every bit of the guilt he'd felt over the last few weeks rushed out. The bitterness of his words made him twist his lips.

As he looked at Evie, her with her clear eyes and conscience, he felt even worse. "You've been nothing but honest," he told her, "from the day I first met you."

"Why wouldn't I have been?" she asked. Confusion filled her words and her face.

He didn't answer. He longed to pace. Even to hide. Andrew wished that this moment hadn't come. Not yet. But those were all foolish things to want. Not things that he could have. Instead, he had to have whatever came out of the situation he'd placed himself in.

Yet he couldn't do it. The words wouldn't come out of his mouth. Instead, what did was, "I can help you. I will protect you and take care of you. What you said, about being alone? You aren't alone, Evie. You have me."

Her smile was sad as she reached a hand out and rested it on his arm. "I appreciate the offer, but I must talk to Mr. Radcliffe. Meaning to or not, I have caused my uncle to take notice of his residence and wealth, and I need to warn him."

"You don't have to," Andrew answered.

Her eyes widened, and she shook her head. "I won't lie, and I won't pretend this didn't happen. It wouldn't do any good. Mrs. Staunton already knows." She wrapped her arms around herself. "I must accept what happens."

"That's not what I meant," Andrew said. He shoved a hand through his hair.

Evie studied him for a moment. "Then I'm afraid I don't understand."

"You don't need to tell Mr. Radcliffe," Andrew explained, then held up his hand to stop the words he knew would come out of her mouth. "I already know."

He could tell she didn't understand and that his words, *I already know,* hadn't fully registered. He pressed on. "I wanted to tell you. A few times I tried to, and something always happened. I'm sorry, Evie. What started off as a misunderstanding grew, and I had no right to do what I did, but for the first time in my life, I had someone like me and want to be with me for myself, not what I could do for them."

She was shaking her head, still looking confused. Andrew took her hands, brought them to his lips for a kiss, and continued. "Evie, what I'm trying to say, what I've been wanting to tell you, is I'm...I'm Mr. Radcliffe. And I'm also in love with you."

Evie stared at him and hastily pulled her hands away. She backed up, stopping only when her spine hit the hallway wall. "You?" she whispered. "You are Mr. Radcliffe?"

Andrew nodded. He felt scared. Miserable. The moment had come, and it wasn't at all how he'd wanted it to be. Instead of a romantic reveal, like out of some sort of story, he'd made a mess of things. He'd been warned, but he'd done it anyway.

Here, she'd been nothing but truthful, and he'd been a liar. He knew better, had always valued loyalty and honesty, yet he didn't give it himself. No wonder she was staring at him. She thought him a hypocrite. And it was true.

"I'm sorry," he said again. "I didn't mean to keep this from you. It was what I was about to tell you when your uncle came. I hope you'll believe me. This whole thing is my fault, but it felt good to be myself. Not someone feared or desired only for his bank account and influence. I don't think I ever had that before. Joe and Mrs. Staunton warned me," he continued. "They found out, and told me it was a mistake. I should have listened. I planned to, but..."

"But you led me on," Evie said, her voice trembling. "Why did you do that to me? What, did you laugh at me behind my back? Did you think I was a fool each time I mentioned Mr. Radcliffe, knowing that I was talking about you?"

The hurt in her eyes was nearly crippling. He longed to pull her into his arms, but knew he'd lost that right. He'd even lost the right to call himself her friend. Right now, Andrew wasn't sure which was worse.

"It wasn't like that at all," he whispered, hoping she'd understand. That she'd listen. Believe him.

Believe a liar? Why would she? His conscience stabbed him. She was far better of a person than he was.

Evie stood there, looking at him. He wished he knew what she was thinking. Her expressions were flickering so quickly, he didn't know which was her dominant emotion and how she was truly feeling.

Andrew swallowed hard. He knew they couldn't stand there forever. He'd said all he could think of to say. But what was she thinking? What would she say when she finally spoke?

There was anger on Evie's face now. She stood, squaring her shoulders, and met his look. There was a hardness to her face. It was nothing less than he deserved, he knew that. It would be a bitter pill to swallow, and Andrew knew he'd never heal from today, but he had to hear it. Had to have her tell him.

"I've heard enough," she said, her words filled with pain. "I'm sure the entire household has." She pushed past him, but in her haste, tripped over his foot.

Without thinking, he grabbed for her. To stop her and to steady her. His hands were on her shoulders, and Evie stilled and looked at him.

"Evie," he begged, "please, say something."

Chapter 19

Evie stood there, nearly frozen in her shock. Today had been too much. She'd gone from being almost deliriously happy at Andrew's kiss to furious at her uncle, then confused and embarrassed, hurt and now angry again at Andrew's admission.

Say something. He wanted her to say something. What could she say? Her heart was hammering, and her legs felt as though they wanted to collapse. The only thing that kept her upright was her pride.

He spoke again, pulling her from her thoughts. "I promise you. I didn't mean for this to happen. I didn't mean to trick you. It was a terrible mistake. It was all my fear and worry about what you might think of me. I'd never make fun of you. You, your opinions, they mean so much to me."

"Mr. Radcliffe," Evie said coldly, and watched him flinch, "likes those who are truthful and loyal. Wasn't that what you told me, Andrew? Yet, he doesn't give the same?"

"I deserve that," Andrew said, his voice low. "It's nothing that I haven't told myself. What I did was wrong, but if nothing else, please believe me that it was never intentional. I never meant to hurt you."

She didn't know what to say. Evie's eyes drifted down the hallway to his study door. The room she'd almost feared. "I used to wonder what you'd be like," she said softly, her gaze still on the door. "What your study was like. Who you were. What kind of a person."

"I'm still the same me," Andrew said. "Only..."

When he stopped, his voice catching, that's when she looked at him. There was pain on his face. Desperation.

Evie shivered and wrapped her arms around herself. Andrew noticed and reached a hand out. He didn't touch her, though. "Please, come to my study. There's a fire. You shouldn't get chilled. You are still weak."

It was only because of the fact that he was correct that Evie nodded numbly and followed him. If this was to be her last day there on the ranch, and make no mistake it would be, she couldn't leave it relapsing in her health.

Andrew pushed open his study door and let her walk in first. Her eyes tried to take in everything at once. She'd been so curious what was behind the heavy wooden door for so long. Now, she finally got to see it. Got to see the place that was his private sanctuary.

The large desk near a window. A sofa, some chairs and a table. Large bookcases stretching taller than her. The scent of horses, and leather, and hay.

The scent of him.

Evie turned and saw him staring at her. She wasn't sure what to say. Right now, she wasn't even sure what she felt. Her emotions were confused. Conflicted.

She still felt worried about her uncle, but now that Andrew knew what had happened, and had sent him away, it felt like there was more time to figure out this situation. Though, she realized she needed to stop calling that man her uncle. They weren't related. She had no one. He'd seen to that. He'd even, in a small way, taken Andrew from her.

Andrew walked in, but stood a distance from her, simply watching as she observed the room. Footsteps from down the hallway caught both of their attentions, and Mrs. Staunton bustled in, carrying a tray with tea and cookies.

"Drink up," she ordered Evie as she set down the tray. "You've had a distressing afternoon, and you are still recovering from your illness." Then, she glared at Andrew. "I knew this would happen. And," she added, "that you'd handle it poorly."

Turning back to Evie, she sighed and met Evie's gaze. "He's dug himself into a hole he's unable to escape from, but I promise you, it wasn't for any reason other than curiosity and love. He cares for you a great deal, and if you are willing to accept his apology, I suspect you two would make a fine couple."

Evie studied Andrew. His cheeks were bright red. "Mrs. Staunton," he began.

"I'm leaving," she said. "You keep apologizing. I told you, you'd better not hurt this girl. I like her." She sniffed loudly and left.

Once she had, gently closing the door behind her, Evie couldn't help but giggle. "I've always been more scared of being on her wrong side than I ever was of meeting Mr. Radcliffe."

"You don't know the half," Andrew said. "She'll scold me like a mother would, never mind I'm an adult." He hesitated then. "But she's right. I've made a terrible mess. I know I have. And I also know I likely can't make it better. But, Evie, please believe me. I'm...I'm still me."

She took a deep breath and closed her eyes. Moments played through her mind. Snippets of his words. The times he'd wanted to tell her something but hadn't been able to. When he'd told her that sometimes, people only wanted someone for what they could give. How, just hardly an hour before, he'd asked whether she really loved him for himself.

Tears sprang to her eyes as sympathy overcame her upset. Poor Andrew. What must it be like to not be loved for yourself, but what you do for others? For that to be the only measure of your merit or worth? But as soon as she asked that question, Evie knew. That's how her uncle had made her feel. And in the end, she'd done so much, and he wasn't even really her uncle. She had so much pain inside of her right now.

"I'm not sure what to do," Evie told him, her voice wobbling. "Not about you, not about my uncle. Not about anything."

"I do," Andrew told her. He stepped close. "I can help you. But first, there's something I need to do."

"What's that?" Evie asked.

"Remember that day we first met?"

"Of course I do," she said, looking at him strangely.

"You shook my hand, and said your name."

"Evie Brown?"

"Yes. And this is what I should have done," Andrew said. He took her hand in his. "Andrew Radcliffe. It's a pleasure to meet you."

She gave a small laugh and shook her head, gently trying to pull her hand away. "You're..."

"I'm what?" he asked, releasing her hand.

Evie smiled. "I'm not sure yet. I need to think about it more." She wrapped her arms around herself again. "I'm worse off than I was a few months ago, Andrew. What will I do? I have nothing now. No money saved, no family. It makes me question everything. Wonder who I really am."

"Take all the time you need," Andrew said. "Just...please don't leave. You aren't alone. You don't have nothing. You have me. Whatever else you need, I can provide. If you'll let me."

"I can't keep my job, not after this. It might bring trouble. People talk." Evie looked down sadly, but raised her eyes when he gently put two fingers under her chin.

"Who cares about your job? I'm asking you to stay with me. I know who you are. That's good enough for me."

"I can't. Aren't you listening to me?" Evie looked at him worriedly.

"I am," Andrew said, moving closer so that their noses were nearly touching, "but you aren't hearing me. I love you, Evie. Every bit of you, from your thoughtful nature to your temper. I love how you were always so concerned for my sake when I did something that you worried Mr. Radcliffe might not approve of. I appreciate so much how you were my friend, how you cared for me. How, I hope, you still care for me."

He leaned forward, and their foreheads touched. "Evie," he whispered, "I want you here. Not as a housemaid. As my wife."

Chapter 20

Something was wrong. Evie was staring at him blankly. Did that mean she hadn't heard him? Or worse, did that mean that she had no desire to marry him? What about their friendship? Had he lost that too?

Andrew felt sick to his stomach. He'd made a mistake. He'd known it all along. Even his most heartfelt apology wasn't enough. He'd hurt the only person who truly loved him for himself.

The longer the silence filled the air, the deeper his stomach sank. He straightened, took a deep breath, and softly said, "Evie? It's...it's okay, if you don't know. If you aren't ready to answer. If the answer is no."

She moved, but not out of his arms. That was a good sign, wasn't it? Evie sighed, then rested her head on his chest. Andrew closed his eyes in relief while simultaneously pulling her closer.

"It's just...I'm scared," she admitted. "I'm me. A no one. With a greedy uncle who isn't even an uncle. Who knows what trouble he might cause? You are a man of great wealth and influence and deserving of a woman who is of the same."

"I disagree," Andrew said, resting his head on top of hers. "What I deserve is you. Actually, no—I don't even deserve your goodness, but I selfishly want it. Want you. Evie, we'll work through this together, in whatever way you want. If you want to try to salvage your relationship with your uncle, we'll do it together, carefully. Your happiness is all I want. Who you are or the people who you know, anyone else's opinion...that doesn't matter to me," Andrew said, holding her close.

"And as for you being a no one?" He pulled back and met her eyes. "You are someone very important to me. You are the other half of my heart. I know this. Without you, I am lonely, and broken, and lost. You complete me, Evie, and you always will. You are something—someone—I never thought I'd have.

"But if you aren't wanting to rush into any sort of relationship, I understand. I'd rather have you as a friend with the hope of something more than to never see your smile or hear your laugh or be with you. I only hope that my foolish mistake didn't cost me that, because for the rest of my life, I will feel the hollow in my soul where you should be."

Andrew continued, "I want you to be my partner in all things, and if it means we wait a while, then that's what we do."

"No," Evie said.

He tensed. No. Of course. He deserved that. Still, a lump formed, and his chest tightened. He loosened his arms around her regretfully, but it was the right thing to do. She didn't want him, and he needed to respect that. Accept the consequences of his actions.

But as he started to step back, Evie grabbed his arms.

"Wait, I don't mean no, no," Evie said.

He stared down at her, every bit of him confused, and she gave a soft laugh while she shook her head.

"I'm sorry. My thoughts are all jumbled. There are so many all at once. But there is one thing I know without a doubt. Today...when my uncle was talking, there was a terrible feeling of loss going through me. Not because of him, but because of what his words and actions meant. That I would have to leave, and likely never see you again."

Evie let her hands rest on his arms, then go up to his shoulders. "I don't want to be without you. So, no. No, I don't need to think about anything. I know what I want. You. I've known it for quite some time now, and I'm just happy you want me as well."

"I do," Andrew said. "There is nothing more that I will ever want." It was true, and his chest felt as though it might explode with joy that she wanted him.

"I just realized something," Evie said, looking up at him with that beautiful smile of hers he adored.

"What's that?" he asked.

"We don't have to go before Mr. Radcliffe to ask permission to court or marry," Evie laughed.

He pulled her close. "What a relief," he joked. "I've heard a good number of things about him. But...I hear that Mrs. Staunton is even scarier."

Her infectious laughter soon had them both gasping for air. Once he'd managed to control himself, he took both her hands into his. "I love you, Evie. That will never change. I'll do my best to always make you happy. So, will you marry me?"

"Yes, I will, Andrew. I love you too," she said with a smile. "And I can't think of anything better."

"You might..." he said, and his eyes lit up. The moment had finally come for him to tell her the surprise he'd been planning. Nerves filled him, and he hoped he wasn't wrong in that she'd like it. What if she didn't? He took a deep breath. It was too late to worry about that now.

"I have a surprise to tell you about. It's something I've been working on. I cannot wait to show you." He released her and went to his desk. Opening a drawer, he pulled out a paper tube and waved it excitedly. "Look!"

Evie stood next to him and studied the large paper he unrolled. She looked at it for a long moment, but finally shook her head in defeat. "I'm not sure what this is. You seem incredibly excited about this. Tell me, so I can be too!"

"It's a building blueprint," he explained, his broad grin nearly splitting his face. His cheeks hurt, but it was a feeling he didn't mind at all. He just hoped she would be excited as well. "This is a thirty-acre plot, about ten miles from here."

"To expand your ranch?" Her head was tilted slightly, her voice and expression curious.

"No, I—we—are opening a home for boys and girls. Building it, hiring teachers who will care for the children and help them to not feel alone. People who can prepare them for life, educate them, teach them skills so they aren't just thrown out into the world."

Evie gasped, and her hands flew to her face. "Do you mean it?"

"I do. You gave me the idea. But I need your help to be sure I don't miss anything. I want you to help me find the best people to work there. I've been corresponding with people for a few days now, making the plans. Within a year, we could have this place built, the staff hired and trained."

"You would do all of this?" Evie whispered.

"I would. Everyone deserves to feel loved, to know that others care for them. To have a home, not just a place they live. They also deserve to be around others who value them and appreciate them for who they are. Not what they can do for them."

Once Andrew said the words, he realized just how much he truly felt them. He knew Evie had felt that loss growing up, and he'd felt it in a similar way, when others only wanted him for what he could do for them. To have a place where children could grow into young adults who felt loved, who felt valued just as they were, no strings attached to their worth...it was something that was sorely needed. Who better to help them experience that than two people who had also felt that way?

Evie leaned close and rested her head on Andrew's shoulder. "I agree," she said. Then, she looked at him. "I hope you feel those things with me. Valued and loved for who you are."

"I do," Andrew said, dropping a kiss on her cheek. "And I'm looking forward to making sure you feel that, too, every day for the rest of our lives."

"With you by my side, I know I will," Evie said.

Andrew searched her face. "I'm sorry for any upset I caused you with my deceit."

"It's quite all right," Evie said. "You have a lifetime to make it up to me."

"I'll do it, too," he promised, meaning every word. It was true. The rest of his days would be spent making sure Evie—and any children who came along to their children's home or their personal home—felt that way too.

Epilogue

Eighteen months later

Andrew nodded in satisfaction as they left the children's home they had built and mounted Starlight and Ginger. Though the school had only been open for a short time, it was already a success. Nearly two dozen boys and girls, ranging from ages four to thirteen, lived there, getting not only their education in school subjects but also life skills.

It had taken just over a year to build the school, and shortly after they were married, it had been completed. Evie had excitedly welcomed each child and staff member on the day the doors officially opened. So far, it was going splendidly.

She'd not heard from her uncle, and Sheriff Steele kept a sharp eye and ear out for the man in case he caused trouble, but Andrew had been helping her research her real family. Perhaps there was still someone out there to connect with, and to feed her longing to know more about the parents she'd never met. Until then, her days were spent with Andrew and all of the others on the ranch, who had quickly, and happily, accepted her.

As they trotted Starlight and Ginger back to the ranch, Andrew mentioned, "I got a letter today I wanted to tell you about."

"From anyone I know?" Evie asked.

"Actually, yes. Remember my friend Kody, who came for dinner a few months ago?"

"I do." Evie nodded. "We showed him the school. It was about to open."

"Well, he wants to secretly fund one as well." Andrew grinned at her.

"Secretly? Why is that?" Evie asked.

Andrew laughed. "Because he's a gambler, remember? Not everyone trusts him, but he's a good man. I'm glad he'll put that money he came into to good use."

"Me too," Evie said. "Where will he open it? Near here?"

"He's found the perfect spot in a little town called Hackberry, Kansas. Another friend of ours lives there. James. A former gunslinger."

Evie laughed. "You know such interesting people. I'm glad we married. It's never dull around you."

"I'm glad you think so," Andrew agreed.

"I do," Evie said. "Do you know what else I think?"

"What?"

"I think I love you."

Andrew grinned as she urged Starlight into a run, and he raced after her. He'd always chase after Evie. Life wouldn't be the same without her.

As the ranch came into view, both horses slowed, and Evie looked over at him. "Home," she said with a smile. "It feels so good to say that, and to know we can give that to others."

"It is," he agreed.

They rode to the barn, and Andrew helped Evie down. She went inside, and when he started to follow, he froze, taking her in. She stood just where he'd seen her for the first time. Only today, she was more beautiful than ever. She wasn't just Evie, she was his Evie. His wife, his partner, and the woman he loved.

"Are you okay?" she asked, a flicker of worry on her face.

"I am," he said, gathering her into his arms. "I have you. Even if I were to lose everything else today, as long as I had you, that's all I'd ever need."

There are other great books in this series as well!

Find all the Weary Hearts and Wounded Spiritsbooks on Amazon!

https://www.amazon.com/dp/B0D3WW5XYZ

Want more? Check out these other stories in Spring Falls.

Asher's Secret

***

The plan? Pretend he's her betrothed and try not to fall in love.

Sheriff Asher Steele doesn't plan to settle down. Not ever. In fact, he avoids the ladies all together. And he doesn't plan to explain why that is. No one's been able to break through the walls of his emotions and that's just the way he likes it.

But when Isabelle Bowman comes to town with a secret of her own, and a heap of trouble following her, he might be the only one who can help her. What he's not counting on is falling in love along the way and considering opening the walls of his heart to protect her.

Running from her half-brother, who desires nothing more than to kill Isabelle Bowman and take her inheritance, she's desperate for a place to hide. Uninterested in marriage, she thinks the sheriff's idea is preposterous. But she's left with no option. With no funds, a sheriff who thinks she's a troublemaker or a liar, and his plan that will never work, she's sure things are not going to end well.

But could they both be wrong about what the future holds?

https://www.amazon.com/Ashers-Secret-Winning-Devotion-Book-ebook/dp/B0CK5GW81M

***

A Sleigh Ride for Charlotte

***

Sometimes the simple choice isn't easy.

Charlotte Harrison dreams of being part of the winter festival, where romance fills the air and new starts are made. Penniless after her family was swindled, she's always stayed home, unwilling to be looked at with pity. But this year Charlotte is desperate and willing to do whatever it takes to be there when she hears the most eligible man in town has his eye on her.

New to town, Dr. Justin Davis is in dire need of someone to assist him at his practice. When Charlotte is suggested, it seems like an opportunity for them both. At first, he simply wants to help her financial situation. But against his better judgment, he falls in love with her. Worst of all, the man she desires is someone he can't stand, and he might have just sent her straight into his arms.

Through a series of surprising events, Charlotte learns that not everyone is as they seem, and when she goes to give her heart away, she's faced with uncertainty. Who is she going to choose? The man she's been longing for? Or the man who truly loves her?

https://www.amazon.com/Sleigh-Ride-Charlotte-ebook/dp/B0CW1JWNNF

Still want more?

Watch for Rosalee's story, May 2025
Watch for Mail-Order Gambler June 2025

***

Read Andrew's friend's story now, in *A Gunslinger for Grace.*

***

She didn't expect a gunslinger to answer her ad. Now, things have gotten complicated. Grace just can't do it alone anymore. When her husband died, he left her with a store to run and two children to take care of. Now, her son is friends with the wrong crowd and her daughter keeps sneaking out. When a string of vandalisms hit her store and the sheriff does nothing, she's more than desperate for help and puts an ad in the newspaper.

James is passing through town after dropping off a criminal at the local jail. A gunslinger by trade, he moves from town to town looking for high-paying work. When he chances upon Grace's ad, the thought of home cooked meals and an opportunity to rest for a while tempts him, and he applies.

No one else wants the job, so Grace reluctantly accepts his offer. But how will a gunslinger be able to help her with her children, the store, and stop the robberies? And why does she feel so drawn to the man who is like no one she's ever met?

https://www.amazon.com/Gunslinger-Grace-Sarah-Lamb-ebook/dp/B0C5FT56DN

Note from Author

Thank you for taking the time to read *To Overcome Betrayal.*

Could I ask for one small favor? Reviews like yours on Amazon mean so much to me and help others to find my books! Even just a single line means a lot!

Also...

Want a FREE book?

Stop by my website to get your no strings attached **FREE book**. It's my gift to you, as a thank you for reading this one.

www.sarahlambbooks.com

About the Author

Sarah is wife to an amazing teacher and mom to two boys. She spends her days working and writing in the Blue Ridge Mountains.

Want more of Sarah's books?

She writes for children and adults! Find them all on Amazon!
https://www.amazon.com/stores/Sarah-Lamb/author/B098H3SGLK

Made in the USA
Columbia, SC
13 February 2025